The Collected Supernatural and Weird Fiction of James Platt

The Collected Supernatural and Weird Fiction of James Platt

Six Short Stories of the Strange and Unusual Including 'The Evil Eye' and 'The Witch's Sabbath'

Tales of the Supernatural

James Platt

LEONAUR

The Collected
Supernatural and Weird
Fiction of
James Platt
Six Short Stories of the Strange and Unusual
Including 'The Evil Eye' and 'The Witch's Sabbath'
Tales of the Supernatural
by James Platt

First published under the title
Tales of the Supernatural

Leonaur is an imprint of Oakpast Ltd

Copyright in this form © 2021 Oakpast Ltd

ISBN: 978-1-78282-906-5 (hardcover)
ISBN: 978-1-78282-907-2 (softcover)

http://www.leonaur.com

Contents

The Seven Sigils

PART 1

BRAVO AND POISONER

The Bottomless Lake of our Legend was reputed an outlet of the Bottomless Pit. No creature of our world had ever swum its lethal ebb and flow, but on the nights of the great Sabbaths, when the wizardry of all Italy swept to its beetling cliffs as to their Holiest of Holies, its waters eructed to the rendezvous the retine of Hell—the wealth of an argosy would not have tempted a Lombard to venture within eye-shot of it after nightfall.

Who, then, are these two men of mortal mould that outstare the depths of the Bottomless Lake itself, and not only that but from the very horns of the Altar of the Black Mass, and not only that, but at the witching hour forsooth of night, when graveyards yawn, and the everlasting doors of Tophet open wide? Their guardian angels of good have surely turned from their right hands, and their evil guardians of the left are grinning from horn to horn.

With the chime of twelve from the distant steeple dies out the last echo of admonition, and they begin to work out such unhallowed errand as alone can have brought them to so damned a spot; the elder of the two in a tone of hushed solemnity addresses a series of questions to the younger, who responds to them with an equally awful gravity, after the manner of a catechism.

"Dost know me who I am?"

"Tosca of Venice, bravo and poisoner."

"And Yourself?"

"Janko the Illyrian, bravo with a right good will, but not yet poisoner."

"My ancestry?"

"Sorcerer stock, whose secrets you would fain have inherited and their trade pursued."

"Why did I not?"

"The Council of Ten bore down upon your race, and but for your extreme youth you yourself would have crossed the Bridge of Sighs. Orphaned By the State, and retaining for sole inheritance the swashing blade that still gnaws at your scabbard, and a few recipes for poisons (which last, however, were worth a Borgia's envy), you soon found yourself compelled to use both the one and the other to buy you bed and board. Proceeding at first with hesitancy, and never sojourning long in one locality, you became by degrees the repository of so many family secrets that at the present day you may stalk assured through the length and breadth of Italy, and ruffle it in what company you will."

"And your own story?"

"I know not by what catastrophe the memory of all my earliest years was shaken loose from me. Suffice it then, that once on a visit to my native country you found me wandering an orphan like yourself, and with a mind so blank that you appropriated it instantly to write on it as it were your own ten commandments. Since that day I have never left you, and I am only repeating what you yourself tell me when I say that you have made me your equal master in every trick of fence. But of that other art of yours that rivals the Creator, my most dutiful entreaties have never availed with you to teach me anything."

"But did I not reasonably argue that you would better attend the heaviness of so terrific a responsibility, until you were of man's estate? And is not today the anniversary of your coming of age? And have we not pelted hither hot-foot from the confines of the land upon that very business?"

"It is true that before entrusting me with even the least of these your ancient awful secrets you have brought me here to-night—for what?"

"To enter you with fitting state upon the beadroll of that

glorious mystery, that with the mere putting on of a glove, or sniffing of a flower can check the most rebellious blood with a thus far shalt thou flow, but no farther!"

"Say, rather to better the assurance that you have of me already from years of fraternal familiar common life, by laying upon me in addition a binding bond ensanctified by centuries of warlock use, and now to be imposed in this very spot where the Master whom thereby we both shall serve is at this hour present, though to us invisible, the Prince of the Power of the Air."

"You are at any rate resolved to link yourself to me with fetters forged in the fire that is not quenched, and by a testament registered in the Chancery of Hell to the effect that any treachery from one of us to the other shall be resented and avenged by that common Master of ours who hears Us at this moment from his postern gate, the Bottomless Lake below?"

"I am resolved to that for which I came here."

"Follow, then, with me the observance of that visible sign and token that unites us in one blood and in one flesh. This horn is from that beast whose form our Master loves to take, when from this altar where we stand, he greets his liegemen and his liege-women turned backward like his prayers. This horn I charge to the half with my own blood, obtained by the biting of my arm. Now do you likewise bite and fill and then drink (to my health) the moiety of the draught so mixed."

"May you live till the Last Trump!"

"You have pledged me in it as I now pledge you, and there remains but one more ceremony. I am about to throw this emptied receptacle into the waters of the Bottomless Lake. You know already that everything that touches its surface, whether living or dead, is forfeit to that Ancient of Days that crouches in wait below. Do you agree that this will be the fate reserved for that one of us two that shall first contravene this super-sacred oath?"

"His soul be the devil's fee."

The emptied horn shot like an elf-bolt into the pathless waters of the Bottomless Lake. The benighted pair that watched it from the unhallowed shrine above could have sworn that a hand came up and caught it as it fell, but a sudden flash of lightning that snapped in their eyes and a peal of thunder that made the four corners of the earth to quake rendered that fact uncertain. The strangers would then have been only too gladly drenched to the skin that they might have hugged their wagered souls in the belief that this unweather was of Nature, and not of the Evil One. But the Heavens shed no tear. There succeeded to that single flash and single peal only the same deadly calm that had preceded them.

Although their business there was over, neither of the two men cared to suggest to the other his secret persuasion that there was no need for further stay. One o'clock whispered from afar its holy amen to their accursed ritual. Other hours flitted by, and still they gazed into unplummeted waves enwrapped in gloom as in their cloaks. At last as it were by a simultaneous impulse they turned together, and with a mutual sigh descended in the direction of the dawning city. From what has been said of the superstitious awe with which the Bottomless Lake was regarded, it will be readily understood that they had to traverse a considerable distance of uninhabited country before coming in sight of the main travelled road.

When at last after the painful up and down of many hills, they perceived the highway cutting through a valley at their feet, the habitual reserve engendered by their profession moved them to await atop the passage of a carriage that appeared in sight in the distance going towards the town rather than continue their journey, and be passed by it.

As it came nearer both these men who had recently drunk so deeply of forbidden founts, suddenly uttered an exclamation that sounded very like a fear. For they saw at the self-same second that the coach contained a girl of beauty beyond a *sultan's* dream, and that some dozen or so of foot-pads darted from both sides of the road and seized the heads of her horses.

The report of a pistol was obviously connected with the fall of the driver like a log from his box. The young lady was left with no other defender than a large black dog that ran behind the carriage, but as the assailants threw the doors open and hustled her out it became apparent that he was chained to the vehicle, and in an instant, they were beyond his reach. But at this critical juncture Tosca descended almost, as it seemed, to the startled abductors with one leap from the heights above, and with a howl like a wild beast.

Although they did not know it, the finest sword player in Europe was in their midst. They went down by couples before him, spitted like larks. They had scarcely grasped the miracle of his presence before the lovely vision of the coach was resting in his left arm (the right still continuing to deal destruction), and she had scarcely glanced at his face, when, with a sigh of evident content with her defender, she hid her golden head in his breast to shut out the shambles from her eyes. But the fight was already past. Half the ravishers lay stretched upon the ground, and the bravo of Venice needed no second or even first glance at them to know that they would never rise again.

The remainder, appalled by a result which they were far from attributing to the purely human agency which had caused it, had only to cast a look beneath his black-a-vised brows, when with a shriek that he was signed in the corner of his eye with the devil's private mark, they precipitately fled. The bravo dropped his sword into its sheath, and now with both arms round her waist he drew the goddess (as she appeared to him) towards her carriage. In doing so he perceived that she had fainted, and printed upon her lips the fiercest as it was the chastest kiss that he had ever bestowed upon woman. By an extraordinary chance (but there was more than chance in it), after completing the foulest rite, he had stumbled upon the purest passion of his life. For no other woman would he have shut the carriage door as he did now after placing her within it, remaining himself outside.

And it is needful to add in this connexion that he had entirely forgotten the very existence of that comrade just bound to him by a tie indissoluble. That comrade, nevertheless, had watched the whole from the altitude where both had first stood. Could he have followed the giddy foothold of his patron he would in that, moment have slain him in his tracks. And that he could in no wise stir from where he stood either previously to take part in that chance medley, or now to snatch a share in the reward of it, was due not at all to cowardice (a thing that must of necessity be unknown to any that followed the fortunes of Tosca), but to a kind, of spell as he fancied that froze him to his place. And of this he was indeed well qualified to judge since he had already experienced the self-same sensation on one (and one only) former occasion.

What puzzled him was that the obvious cause in the prior case was a certain amulet of unknown antiquity and power, which Tosca was accustomed to wear round his neck upon a chain of gold, and which in a moment of confidence he had shown that once to his pupil. Whereas on the present occasion the cause of his vertigo could scarcely be the same, the talisman being invisible. And yet the effect was identical. If anything, more than another had been the actual moving cause of his present icy chill it must certainly be the damsel of the coach. So unmistakeable was the hold which the mere sight of her had taken upon him, that at the instant when Tosca placed his lips upon hers (and they had never been touched before by man), the surging up of jealousy burst the shackles of the spell, and the Illyrian clattered down like an avalanche.

He reached the road at the important moment when his oblivious partner, after shutting the door of the coach, was upon the point of mounting the box to drive the young beauty he knew not whither. Nor did it occur to him that he knew not. But at this precise juncture his dream was shattered by the advent of the Illyrian flashing fires of jealous heat from his eyes. So choked with it was he that he could not speak, but only pointed with one hand to the carriage while he clenched the other in Tosca's face.

The Venetian was equally taken aback by the sudden resurrection of one whose presence in the world he had totally overlooked. How long they would have stared at one another had nothing intervened it would be impossible to say. They were heedless of the barking of the black dog, since that had continued without intermission from the first irruption of the bidstands. But they were twitched bolt round in the direction of the coach by a sudden crack of its wheels. Whether the coachman had fallen from his box through a genuine belief that he was hurt; or whether through an equally genuine desire not to be; or, lastly, through collusion did not appear, but it was sufficiently obvious that the fellow had not received a scratch.

Concluding the danger to be over he had now quietly reassumed his post, and was driving off. He took no more notice of the other two than if he had not seen them (which again might really have been the case), and used his whip to such good purpose that the vehicle was lost to sight (to memory dear) before the rivals had taken a step to arrest its progress. Then burst the storm of mutual recrimination. Tosca first spoke.

"Darkness and devils! You have robbed me of that for which I would not leave whole the skin of any man alive."

"'S death, kinsman, would you draw on me? Remember you not the oath of some few hours ago? Are you already so anxious to tap at that postern we both wot of? Knock then, and it shall be opened unto you. Ho, you pale at this reminder, and suffer your hand to drop from the hilt of that ancestral spit of yours."

"You were well advised to speak before I had drawn, or you would perchance have learned ere this that there are one or two tricks of fence I never taught even to you."

"Deceit upon deceit You have always given me to understand that there was absolutely nothing in that branch of our partnership that you had not revealed to me. Perchance I shall ere long come upon some other tit-bit churlishly rapt aside. But why do I chide you for teaching me too little, when I had rather cause to weep salt tears that you have fathered me too much? When you met me, I had, as you have told me oft, a mind so blank that you could write on it (and that was the attraction that led you to adopt me) whatever kind of script you chose; And you chose to scribble the Devil's A, B, C.

"It is through your corruption of my innocent youth that I am unfit today to even look upon such as she who has just escaped us (and there ruled her favouring star). And if you reply that you have kept me till I was of age, unspotted from the worst half of your villainies, I dare swear that I should not be far out in conjecturing that regard for the safety of your body, rather than for that of my soul, was the true reason why you have never yet suffered me to wear the glass mask in your laboratories. And, to crown all you kissed her."

"Did I kiss her? I thought it was a dream."

Thus, Tosca murmured softly to himself, his head falling upon his breast, as if in communion with some saint. It was Janko who this time broke the silence by clutching of his sword. But Tosca looked up with a glance so diabolical, that he dropped it again at once. By a motion of his hand, the Venetian, as it were compelled him to seat himself by the side of the road; and, sitting quietly beside him, commenced in the following strain:—

"You make me laugh apart when you speak of my corrupting your innocent youth. If you only knew; the truth! Or, as you said just now. (God knows whether inspired by good or evil chance), if you only knew that titbit rapt aside, as you thought, churlishly, (when you merely guessed at it), but in reality with more generosity than you will be decently able to thank me for (when you only know the facts). Your, innocent youth, indeed!! By the God above us, whom we both fear, and neither serves, you will see by the story I am about to tell you that I knew all the time, and as I say with generosity have concealed from you, the nature of that catastrophe that shook loose from you the memories of all your earliest years. You will see that before your mind became a blank, I had read upon it (tender as were your years) the lurid brand of Cain.

"You will see that your brain was seared by your own atrocious hand, and that my adoption of you afterwards was based on the calculation that for a bravo and poisoner there could be in the whole round world no better raw material than a matricide! Start not till you have heard me out. I was in Illyria, reasons which your experience of ups and downs, in our profession will readily enable you to appreciate had caused me to retire (rather hurriedly, I confess) from the town which I had honoured with my presence for some months. The same reasons oblige me to travel in preference by night, and to secrete myself by day. On the first occasion of my doing this latter, I settled upon an apparently deserted hut in the trackless depths of the forest.

"This hut consisted of a large front room (reaching to the roof tree) for the accommodation of the two-footed, and a stall at back for that of the four-footed creation. The latter did not run so high as the front room, inasmuch as it contained a loft for fodder atop, and it was in this airy apartment that I decided to take my siesta, since it had openings both upon the stables (if I may so call it) and the front chamber, and my disposition as you know is strategic. I had slept, I know not how long, when I was awakened by a noise in front, and speedily ascertained that it was caused by an altercation going on among visitors to the parlour. Do not start till you have heard me out.

"One of the disputants was yourself. The other, who occupied the only stool in the place, was a grey-haired, blear-eyed female of considerable antiquity. I know nothing of your accursed Illyrian jargon. But without understanding the conversation I could see the *beldame* hugging to her withered breast a jewel, small, but of great price, and withal slung upon a golden chain. I tell you without hesitation that it was the same amulet you have been shown by me upon a previous occasion, foolishly as it happened, since it stirred you so profoundly as to almost resurrect your buried remembrances. That it came into the hands of your precious dame by some feat of robbery I have no doubt whatever. How it came into mine you will presently see.

"Your excited gesture, as it seemed to me, might afford me some clue to the progress of the quarrel, which I presumed had arisen as to the fate of your booty, but I had scarcely awakened up sufficiently to pull my reasoning faculties together, when the whole thing ended in an, even to me, unexpectedly horrible manner. You suddenly pushed a pail (which stood hard by) beneath the back of the unsuspecting crone, and flashing a hanger from under your rags you swept off her grey head into the bucket with the single shearing stroke of a seasoned cut-throat. Then throwing upon the floor the glittering bauble of contention, you surprised me still more by swiftly separating the hands and feet, then the arms at elbow, and the legs at knee, then the stumps from the trunk, and finally the trunk itself into smaller parcels.

"That moment, and today, are the two occasions of my life upon which I have loathed my calling. By my word and oath, I was as sick as a dog upon the litter of your loft. When I looked again you had cast down the weeping steel which had been the unwilling instrument of your crime. Packing all the sections in a kind of bag or sack you rolled it up compactly. Then seizing the ensanguined pail in the hand that was not occupied by that pitiful truss of what had just been humanity, you strode with them both from the desecrated home, but how you disposed of your burdens I neither know nor care. That you had loaded your conscience with a grislier deed than it could bear, I soon had good reason to know.

"Perturbed at my perturbation I had scrambled to *terra firma*, and had recovered myself sufficiently only to secure that amulet (which as you know I still wear), when you re-entered empty handed in that same state of idiocy, which moved me to overcome my distaste for associates and adjoin you to myself in my profession. Besides, I could not but admit (when once more fully myself) that you had shown for it considerable vocation."

The face of the Illyrian rolled with beads of sweat. For the third time he was bound hard and fast by that same fascination which already twice before had enthralled him. And as each time before so again it was for a different cause. The first of these two prior occasions resulted, as we know, from the sighting of the amulet. The second on the sighting of the divinity of the coach. But this third time was again different from the other two, in this respect, that (although he would not have confessed it for all the riches entombed in earth) he had now fully recognised the reason and connexion of all three. He rose deliberately and spoke:—

"Now, you have told me, to suit your own purposes, a certain amount of the truth, I remember to your confusion the details you intentionally omitted. You lie in your throat when you say that when I re-entered that room, I was in the vacant state already. I re-entered that room (and you know it) as sane as when I left it. I found you standing there prepared with a glib story to the effect that you were a stranger just stepped into the hut with

16

the view of seeing whether it was inhabited or not by anyone who could serve you as a guide through the forest. Not knowing you so well as I do now, I was simple enough to believe you. It never entered my head that you could have witnessed the drama that had just been played, nor did I think of the talisman in my momentary confusion at seeing in the place a foreigner.

"I have now no doubt but that if I had looked for it I should not have been able to find it. You diverted my attention by inviting me to quaff from your spirit flask on the plea that I looked unwell, as in truth I might, after the ordeal I had just passed through. In my innocence (for I was innocent) I accepted the draught, and the drug which you had placed in the liquor beforehand destroyed my memory, never to return, until this eventful day.

"Yet I think there was, however, one former occasion which it just missed a return. That was when you showed me that ill-omened amulet, and it awakened in me sentiment inexplicable then, but which now I am no longer at a loss to understand. That jewel was wrought by the science of my kinswoman, in whose hands you surprised it—for my people, too, were of the ancient religion, like your own, and sorcerers of the Black Side."

At the commencement of this speech, Tosca seemed momentarily disconcerted, but, as it continued, this sentiment was succeeded by something very like prostration, and when he replied it was with reverence.

"What a galliard this is, and how aright I guessed when I saw in him the making of a master in my trade. I thought to dash him with my revelation of a monstrosity among crimes. I was a fool, indeed, to think that a younker would bleach over the dissection of a granny, who had anointed him from his cradle with the grease of unbaptised babes. But I failed, and there's an end on't, and now sheer steel must decide the issue, for we meet on equal ground. Equal do I say? Nay! the boy is my superior in callousness, for I dearly loved my own old people, though I never say God rest their souls."

He rose, and both men laid their hands upon their hilts. One of them had not very long to live. But before entering upon the fateful lists, the Illyrian turned to speak again.

"In case you slay me, which I believe will not be the case (for God does sometimes defend the right), I cannot forbear an answer to your last taunt. You did not understand, and you have never understood, and you never will understand the real meaning of the scene you saw enacted in that room upon that day. I am not sure whether it was a blessing or a curse upon our race that you did not catch the drift of our remarks in our native language, which you contemptuously term jargon. Had you done so the fate of all three of us would have been better or worse, but at any rate far different.

"The tortures of the Inquisition would not force from me the secret, which was confided to me then by that ancient lady whom you saw me slay indeed, but only after her own repeated prayers and instructions. I shudder to think what has become of her remains which she entrusted to my pious care, and which for your accursed interference I have been unwillingly prevented from attending to. I know, indeed, the fate of her other legacy (for the amulet was a legacy that you thought a theft); but it is now too late (again through your accursed interference) for me to make such use of that knowledge as she had enjoined upon me to do.

"But to you (who know nothing of its use and profit) it shall hang as a millstone round your neck, and whether you live or whether you die it shall infallibly sink you now or hereafter to the undiscovered bottom of that Bottomless Lake whose source we both do know. And whichever of us falls shall by the terms of that enactment (of so short a while ago) be resented and avenged by that Master of ours, who waits even at this moment for that most unhappy man."

The face of Tosca became white and red. He flashed that time-honoured blade of his from its sheath, and motioned with it to the Illyrian to take up a position opposite to him. Janko turned round for one second to do so, and in that second the sword of his faithless foe was plunged remorselessly through his back. The point protruded through his breast. The next instant the sword had been withdrawn, and the Illyrian lay upon the turf among the ragged hedge pirates, who had fallen before by the same trained hand. But this time the Venetian took the trouble to assure himself of the death of his foe before returning his sword to its bed. That was the only honour he paid to the body that had once been only less dear to him than his own.

That done, he threw himself down at the road side, and took out from under his doublet that very talisman of which we have heard so much. It had gained greatly in his estimation by the mystery which had lately thickened round it. We have already mentioned that it was suspended round his neck by a gold chain; but we must now give a more particular description of the gem itself. It had undoubtedly originally been intended for a seal, or, to speak more correctly, seven seals, for it had (and this constituted its particularity) seven sides or facets, and on each of these engraved a sigil or cabalistic monogram, and each sigil was that of a different planet of the seven that rule over the seven days of the week. All this the bravo, from his early environment, was sufficiently skilled to know.

He also recognised at once that the person wishing to use the stone for its original purpose of sealing, would choose on each day that facet of the gem which bore the signature of the planet that presided over the day in question. But this, though no doubt of considerable efficiency, was not by any means of so great virtue as to sufficiently explain the very enigmatical manner in which the amulet had been alluded to by the hapless boy, whose present fate he shuddered to reflect on. He endeavoured, with more or less success, to banish speculation on that point by returning to his examination of the ring, if we may apply that term to a jewel which was not pierced with sufficiently large a hole to fit even upon the smallest of fingers.

Such hole as it had, and through which its chain now passed, he conjectured must have been originally intended to receive the handle of the seal, upon which, fitting loosely, the gem turning round and round could be made to present any facet desired to the paper which its owner intended to impress. At this point of his meditation the bravo was aroused by the sound of footsteps. A number of officials, both on horse and otherwise, had arrived from the neighbouring town. These he recognised at once as belonging to that inconvenient class (the guardians, let us say, of public safety) from whom he had fled on many another well remembered occasion besides the one he had just made mention of in his story to the ill-starred Illyrian.

Yet at the present moment he had no fear of them. Perhaps this was because he knew that they came on account of the depositions of the lodestar of his dreams, and that he would have run any risk to be brought once more into chain with her. A less hardened adventurer might have been embarrassed by the presence of Janko's body. But to a fertility of resource such as Tosca had needs acquired, it presented no obstacle whatever. He rose, and bowed with a grace he had learned in the very highest society. The officers returned his salute. They conjectured rightly that this stranger of distinguished appearance was the beaten blade who had performed the prodigies of valour, which when told them in the city they had deemed to be fabulous, but of which they now saw the proofs before their eyes. The obliging champion was quite willing to relate his own private version of the affair. He paused only to consider whether it would be advisable to have been wounded slightly, but he decided against this fiction as liable to lead to trouble.

"Yes; as you say, I naturally wished to rest awhile after the fatigues of such a combat. Besides, I guessed, of course, that I should soon see upon the field of battle you gentlemen of justice, whose promptness in these matters has become proverbial, and with whom I would not for the world have lost the chance of an interview. I might, it is true, have foisted myself into the carriage for its journey to town. But the lady, as she doubtless told you, had fainted right away, and I was therefore debarred from obtaining that permission, without which no man of breeding could venture to take such a liberty. And before I had time to achieve a seat on the box, the coachman was off; for the fellow was drunk, as your penetration must have perceived from the muddled state of his evidence.

"Of the valour you so kindly allude to, my modesty forbids me to speak. But I am bound in honour to temper your flattering opinion of the achievement by confessing that I am a fencing master by profession, and that a score or so of thrusts and parries is merely a matter of daily bread with me. I must add, in this connexion, that I am also a physician, and one possessed of medicaments that cure all ills. Further, I was proceeding to your town with the view of establishing a dual practice among you, when this trifle we are discussing fell athwart the even tenor of my way, and I hope still to establish myself there, and even to continue my journey in your company (which is such as I most affect) now this accident has given me, as I perceive, introduction to all the most desirable connexions in the place.

"You will notice yonder, by the way, a fellow of better apparel than the rest of the run-a-gates, and whom I take to be their captain. The other *scaramouches* gave me no trouble whatever, but I must confess that the *spadassin* in question was a little bit more of a customer. I had the lady on one arm (as she doubtless told you), and had the rabble been able to get on all sides of me at once, the affair would indeed have been the devil's delight. But since I kept my back, like an old campaigner, to the coach, I felt no kind of flurry; and, as I knew from the first that I should, I came at length to disarm him.

"The poltroon then turned to save his skin (I had thought him braver stuff); but I, as you may suppose, was far too limber for him, and skewered him through the back. You can see for yourselves how my point protruded through his breast. In my humble opinion he might well dance in chains here on a gibbet upon the scene of his crime, as a warning to the rest of his riff-raff that scuttled away from my invincible arm as soon as their leader fell."

This Tosca considered the master-stroke of his dissimulation. No suspicion could now light upon him. The lady had seen but him, and knew nothing of his companion. The coachman had either seen two men or none. If he spoke of two, they would ascribe it to his drunkenness, and inquire if he did not also see two ladies. Tosca was furthest of all from suspecting that by this very suggestion he thought to be so masterly he was forging the bolt that should destroy him. With delight he perceived that the officers had clutched at his idea, and immediately set their underlings to work upon the gallows, after first entombing the raggeder ruffians ignominiously in a ditch.

Leaving them to their congenial work Tosca proceeded with the officers to town, and gathered as he went all the particulars that he could of his enchantress. And her name, which he heard for the first time, seemed familiar as a household word. Vergilia had resided for months in the city, but was by birth a stranger, from what country no one knew. It was only known that she had sojourned for similar periods in other principal places. She was an orphan, she was unmarried, she was an heiress. Wherever she pleased to set her wandering feet men flocked in shoals to be trampled beneath them.

And of these, Tosca shrewdly guessed, were the majority of his present companions. She consistently refused all offers, and this was the unanswerable argument of the more logical sex to their women, who hated her like poison, and who would have it that she made use of love philtres to effect her endless conquests. The only ground for this assertion seemed to be that wherever she travelled her bed chamber was always sacredly reserved to her own person, entered by no one else under any circumstances whatever, and locked when she was not within, she herself performing all domestic duties connected with it

Those admirers of hers, who had not yet put their fate to the touch, all indignantly scouted the theory advanced by the rejected that she concealed a lover in this sanctum. Nor was such an idea surely possible to anyone who looked with unjaundiced eye, even once on her virginal purity. Tosca gazed on her for the second time that day, and swore within his heart of hearts (quite drowning all recollection of that prior oath) that the very first lover she should have would be none other than himself.

PART 2

THE DEVIL'S CANDLE

The revolution of our legend brings us once more, round to that same direful boundary hour, with which it was commenced between midnight and the first born of the day. But on the hills a gibbet stands that stood not there before, a beacon to the minions of the moon. Alas for the misguided youth that hangs there helpless and unhouseled. His brave attire the cupidity of his topsmen had appropriated to their own use. His body they had arrayed for the sake of decency in rags stripped from the verminiferous trunks of his several supposed followers, and these huddled him like the swathings of some dismantled mummy. A gorged carrion bird dozes upon each of his shoulders. The hinds, whom their business brought upon the road even so late as twilight, had run afield copiously crossing themselves.

Who, then, is this—a woman, too—that comes at the awfullest hour of all, and to the very foot of the gallows? Nothing but her eyes can be seen from under her hood. Are those the eyes of Vergilia that Tosca dreams of and deems unfathomable as the Bottomless Lake itself? Is the intuition of her sex, then, unfailing after all, and she a witch, that with love philtres works her syren spell, and seeks at this dread hour for the wherewithal? And what, then, can she peer for about the foundations of a gibbet, save alone that fetid and fearsome white flowered orange berried Devil's Candle mandragora that is engendered in the womb of earth from a gibbeted murderer's drippings on the midnight of his death?

The Illyrian bravo had been seven times a murderer (if not seventy times seven), and many a lost soul rejoiced in Hell that night over the weird that the witch woman was to work. She has found it at last, the favourable specimen, by her long sought through fruitless years. She has found the root in human form complete—two armed, two legged—the Microcosm caricaturing man. And now her low whistle brings her black hound forward out of the black night. Even she is affected as she kisses him for the last time. Iscariotical kiss! With a cord from her youthful waist she attaches animal and plant together, and flees from thence, stopping her ears as she runs.

The hound (whose faith is to strike his death-knell) seeks to follow her. and finds himself held back. He wrestles with the invisible obstacle and conquers, but to die, for as the unholy mannikin root is perforce torn out of its mother earth it utters a piercing shriek that makes rattle the chains of its father above, and the hound, in an instant foaming at the mouth, in fits expires. Then, and then only, turns the murderess back on her blood-stained steps. The carcase of her sole unvenial follower she casts falteringly apart. The girdle is already attached by one end to the gruesome plant. By throwing round to it the other end she completes the circuit of her shapely throat, and held fast by this improvised necklace tucks the loathsome herb creature into her lovely bosom, which no being of its sex had ever yet been free of. Hence now to develop him, for to this is that secret chamber destined that had never seen denizen but herself before.

There is her laboratory, and there shall this earth child be magically tendered and nourished, and most magically grow to more and more of man's resemblance. Since in a manner by his mystical birth he is one flesh and blood with the murderer that begot him, he is perforce of Hell, and can Hell's secrets impart to the enchantress that holds him in her power. To what her cravings tend, which by his means or any other that affords itself, she must and will by hook or crook attain, we now shall shortly see. In spite of her evident youth, Vergilia was far too accomplished an actress, of course, to reveal by word or sign her secret studies to the gilded youth that continue to throng her halls.

But Tosca visited her upon a different footing. Spending his days with her in the body, and his nights with her in the spirit—spacing out with drink and dice the unutterable intervals when he could do neither one nor the other—he neglected his professional avocations altogether, and existed absolutely for her. On her part she had shown him, as we have seen, particular favour from the first moment she saw him, and this became continuously more and more after she had wormed his story from him—as much as he chose to tell, and which of course excluded entirely the existence of the Illyrian—until at length she requited him with like confidence.

What the butterflies that sought their own purposes about her chose to think of her preference she cared not, but her modesty at length obliged her to account for it in private to the preferred one himself by alleging the similarity of their descent (for that she also came of old necromantic stock), and to explain her refusal of all suitors (even to coronets) on the grounds that none of them could satisfy, till Tosca came, her yearnings for the occult. To an arch image alone would she give her right hand, and his right hand she meant to be. The blessing of the Church would be a curse to such a pair. Heedless then of what, in their position, they needs must deem the degradation of any such ceremony, she had herself devised her own test piece by which a favoured suitor could be at the same time tried, and by its failure or success dismissed or indissolubly wedded.

She had sworn in fact to bestow herself without reserve upon the student (his person being also to her fancy) who could call up for her substantial from the vasty deep a magical palace in which her fantastic imagination had long run riot, and in which carnal love and cabalistic lore should wander hand in hand the livelong day without let or hindrance from the outer world well lost. Prone to such thoughts from her cradle, this aerial architecture of hers had taken final shape in the first days of her visit to that town, when disdaining the legend of the boors, she had penetrated the precincts of the Bottomless Lake, and quickened her brain with the idea of how suitable to a lover and his mistress would be retreat into a never-visited seclusion such as that.

Then the thing grew. She pictured and demolished one after another various enchanted buildings floating upon the waters themselves (and that was the common thread that ran through them all) sailing to the shore upon the wish of the dwellers in them, but entirely inaccessible to any outward authority, either human or divine. Now that she had discovered the Venetian to be the one man to whom she would accord permission to substantialise her dreams (supposing he could find the power) she submitted to him with much shy laughter her latest ground plan of this castle in the air. She had borrowed from the sensuous East its keyhole arches and quadrangular bowers built round, and enclosing court yards glowing with flowers from every region of the earth, and never the same at two successive visits.

Birds interchanged at every inspection in like manner were to agitate the air with their antiphonies. And the fountains in the centres of all the court yards (fed from the waters of the Bottomless Lake) when lapped into the beakers of the lovers would become the rarest wine. The outermost waters would glister with gold and silver fish, shot through with the plungings of white aquatic birds. Within the building, the rooms kaleidoscopically should never meet them twice with the same face. Their servants should be automata scattered through every chamber, and ready at a touch to fly to master or mistress like *genii* of the Arabian Nights, but instantly relapsing after service into their first stony insensibility.

Of much more Vergilia whispered such as at times frenzied in Tosca the knowledge of his impotence to win her upon her terms. Had he but inherited the secrets of his fathers! Had he but the knowledge stored up in the grey brain of that hairless blear-eyed Hell-sent hag of Illyria! Could he but solve the enigma of the Seven Sigils, that at any rate might bring him somewhat nearer to his end! And his rivals envied him. Closer and closer there seemed to flutter to him the moth they thought he had singed. But never close enough.

Then came an event that led up to his climax of fruition found green in the mouth. Stated in short, it fell somewhat as follows: At the end of her daily banquet she was wont to leave her guests to their wine, while she paid one of her frequent visits to that unseen chamber. One of those disappointed suitors of hers (as it chanced, or was fated on a certain day), inspired with the valour of much wine imbibed after she had left her table, swore roundly that he would follow her, and pluck out at any hazard the heart of that mystery. Before he could be stopped by fellow guest or flunkey, he had stumbled up the stairway, and burst open the door she had but lately closed behind her.

The next moment a most frightful shriek resounded through every corner of the house. It was not Vergilia's. It was uttered by the foolhardy intruder. The company started from their seats. But before they could do anything, he staggered into the room again with hair as white as snow, and lips that gibbered loathsomely. Amid a scene of indescribable confusion, he was carried off by his friends insane and impenetrable as to the cause of his fright, nor did he ever recover sufficiently to give an explanation of it. When all the rest of the terrified crowd of loungers and lackeys had hustled pell-mell from the house, Tosca alone remained. His hour he thought had come. But it was only in a measure so.

The lady of the house re-appeared, it is true, after the hurried exodus of masters and servants, and agitated as he had expected, but not to his surprise by their defection. She babbled brokenly, instead, of someone else whom she had lost through the unexpected intrusion of that venturesome drunkard, now sobered for good and all. Thus, she rooted from that moment in the mind of Tosca the horrible suspicion that the story of the concealed lover might have some truth in it after all. How could he know aught of her experimental mandrake culture, for of course it was the mandrake she referred to? The only creature besides herself that had witnessed her infernal arcana had just been borne a mouthing maniac from the seat of her operations, and perhaps not even had time enough to notice the nature of the disaster, which his untimely interference had brought about.

However, for the time Tosca dismissed his suspicions when she fell into his arms and telling him between laughter and tears that he was now the only hope that remained to her, she begged him at once to summon together all his scattered occult acquirements, and make an incantation that very night that should yield them both their heart's desire. He swore to do so, hardly knowing what he swore, and fled from her in a wind of excited passion and passionate resolve. For some time after this he endeavoured to put his ideas coherently together by dint of pacing madly through the streets. It was already dusk, and at first, he elicited no remark.

But presently he noticed that his footsteps were being dogged. He was a connoisseur in such matters. This must be a rival more fixed than the remainder of the craven herd that had so readily taken flight, and one that had watched the bravo during the time that he stayed behind. Or perchance nothing more mysterious than a dunning creditor, for Tosca had lately run out of ready money, and while exercising no trade still maintained a splendid appearance. Nor had this also been altogether without weight with him when he accepted the challenge of his bewitching mistress. Not wishing to embroil himself with the person whom he supposed to be shadowing him, he entered a tavern and called for wine. He had scarcely seated himself when a masked stranger of short stature and somewhat uncouth appearance entered the same inn, and sat down at the same table, giving the same order.

The nerves of our Venetian were more shaken by the extraordinary episode of the afternoon than he would himself have cared to own. Not liking the looks of his would-be boon companion, and conjecturing some connexion between that individual and the counter of his paces, Tosca got up and left the tavern without awaiting the execution of his command. To his consternation the stranger followed him. An exciting chase ensued. The bravo entered house after house, seating himself in each case, and always closely hugged by his mysterious hanger on, who as regularly seated himself by the bravo's side, and as soon as he withdrew followed him out into the street.

A kind of panic seized the fearless swordsman. A challenge to the inexplicable stranger stuck again and again in his throat. At last the houses began to close their shutters. The baffled fugitive struck desperately out of the town into the open country, and made his way in the direction of the Bottomless Lake. As the footfalls of his ghostly visitant pattered still behind him, he consoled himself with the grim reflection that right up to that ill-omened shore, at any rate, the spy would not dare to venture. But he was mistaken. As he paused breathless on the brink of that Stygian sea and faced round boldly on to what he deemed to be invisibility, he found it was instead the form of his fear that stood there as before. He was seized with the boldness of desperation, and addressed the mysterious and still masked being with a voice of tolerable calm.

"Who are you, and what is your need of me?"

"I am Magloire, a necromancer of France, and it is you that have need of me."

"You are over bold to say so."

"I say what I know. Dare you deny that you entertain the

28

intention of making an incantation here this very night, and that you lack only the means to do so? A scheme of geomancy acquainted me with your design, and being entangled in your fate, for reasons that you must not know (for you will know them if anything too soon) I sped from afar upon wings of wind to conduct your conjuration for you."

"You have a price for this?"

"I see you are a man of the world, and are aware that nothing is usually given for nothing. I ask you merely to sign this bond."

"I understand your interest in me better than you seem to think, and on no account will I barter away my immortal soul."

"Your immortal soul, do you say? By the Nine Legions of Hell, does the man think that the cross was stretched on Calvary for any such scum as he? Your immortal soul, of which you hug yourself the possessor, was lost irredeemably from your cradle up. The signature to the bond is a matter of form."

"You do not think so since you ask me to sign it. But ask of me anything else, and it shall be given to you."

"By the tie of which I spoke, that is stronger than blood as blood is thicker than water (so they say), I will help you, though you vouchsafe me a mere keepsake. Make over to me that amulet that you wear around your neck, and the bargain is firm and true. The dawn shall caress a tenement based on the shifting foundation of these waters, such as even shall satisfy the caprices of Vergilia."

The bravo had recovered himself, as we have said, but these evidences of an intimate knowledge of his affairs filled him again with apprehension. And the stranger still continued masked. After a short deliberation, however, Tosca decided not to let slip an opportunity as welcome as unexpected, and granted apparently in exchange for a trinket of no worth to him whatever, though he was not unaware that it might be of inestimable value to anyone who knew (as this Frenchman presumably did) the secret of the Seven Sigils. With a parting sigh for its enigma still unsolved, so often the toy of his leisure hours, he detached it from his neck, and passed it on to the Gaul, who fastened it about his own. That he was a wizard of his word became immediately apparent. Taking up a piece of chalk he scored out rapidly a double circle, one circumference within the other, upon the shelf of rock upon which they stood.

Between the two circumferences he drew a ring of symbols of purport to the Venetian unknown, but which he endeavoured to retain in his memory for possible future use. Within the innermost of these two lines of defence the sorcerer collected a quantity of brushwood, and after having ignited these materials he entrusted the bravo with sundry perfumes, some in the shape of evil smelling dried stuffs, and some sealed up in phials, with minute instructions as to the order and quantities in which (the incantation having commenced) they were to feed the fire. To Magloire would fall the duty of reciting the continuous charge which for the whole duration of the work was to hold the evil angels in thrall.

Lastly, the Gaul drew his companion's attention to the fact that as soon as midnight sounded the conjuration was to commence, and before one must end. For that hour alone would signatory protectors avail him against the furies he evoked. But this Tosca already knew. He was, as we have seen, no such novice in the worship of powers retrograde as this schooling showed his colleague to believe. The distant clock now struck (how well the bravo remembered all the circumstances in which he had heard that sound from this spot before), and the sorcerer began in a thunderous voice to recite his litanies. Couched throughout in somewhat dubious Latinity they were by the bravo only partially understood, but he perceived that commencing with, extravagant bead roll of the Heavenly, powers with which they two had fortified themselves, and with, impudent encomiums, of their own matchless courage and endurance among men, Magloire proceeded to eulogise the nine princes of the lower world in terms the most complimentary, exhorting them to satisfy their good friends the exorcists in the mere trifle they demanded.

As this modest request was not responded to, the reciter gradually changed his tone. The compliments became thinned by degrees and beautifully less, and were fairly well mixed with horrible threats, and opprobrious epithets, which again meeting with no recognition, the theme of the chant now ceased to contain any allusion whatever of a gratifying character. All was menace piled on menace and insult piled on insult, Pelion upon Ossa till the riotous whirl of words merged into one continuous curse, in the midst of which reverberated again and again (amid the shudders of the waters and the trembling of the earth) that ineffable sacred and secret Name of Names, at which the celestials and the terrestrials and the infernals do shake together and are troubled and confused.

And with that there rumbled thunders round the skirts of earth and belched forth lightnings from their midst. And the lightnings continued to lighten without pause, until they seemed all one meteor of fire that hovered over the surface of the Bottomless Lake. And the meteor burst and shot forth myriads upon myriads of shapes less forms down towards the surface, whilst upwards from the surface rose a sort of scum or mist. And this scum or mist, meeting those shapeless forms, they seemed to seize upon it—and work it—and make it build as it were wails. But all was seen as through a glass darkly, and, besides, the bravo was still employed in casting priceless balsams upon hissing flames that many a time and oft became half extinguished (to his terror) by the sweat that rained from his brow.

By his side the French enchanter still swayed his arms towards on high, and on high unceasingly rolled his incomprehensible cabala. The slightest fear or the slightest hesitation, and what might not be their fate? For such a slip, innumerable infernal skirmishers were hovering hard by in readiness. But now the danger is almost over. The gangs have done their grudging work, and a palace hangs between wind and water seductive and serene where nothing hung before. The last odours are burning. The weird wailing of the magus is slackenings into the majestic formulae of dismissal. Without this termination to the ritual the magicians on leaving their sanctuary would have been torn limb from limb by the awaiting fiends. But being expelled as ceremoniously as they had been evoked, the filmy hosts had no choice for it but to crumble into the nothingness from which they came.

"Go in peace unto your place! Peace be between you and us! Be you ready to come when you are called."

These culminating words of the oration were uttered at the very moment that the faithful distant watchman proclaimed it the hour of one. As the two daring trespassers upon realms forbid stepped out from their double breastwork, the bravo in vain endeavoured to make out the exact architectural details of his palace in the darkness. It was pretty clear to him, however, that instructions given had been faithfully fulfilled. He considered that he had done a very good night's work How unexpected when he left Vergilia's house was this chance rencounter that fate had in store for him. He began to have some regard for Providence. He paid no attention to the wizard who was commencing to obliterate his signs.

Magloire had done his work well, but he had been paid for it in advance. So much for Monsieur Magloire (of France), who, he presumed, would now be off again about his own affairs. Tosca strolled towards the city. His business was to wait upon his betrothed (for such she now surely was), and drag her off at once to the castle of her behest. A day of luxury followed by a night of love. That was his bill of fare. But he had reckoned without his host. He was ignorant that, in exchange for the palace, he had bartered the true key to the situation and most stringent claim of all upon the regard of his Vergilia. He was far from suspecting that essential clue to the labyrinth which Janko had recovered only just before his death, but which world without end would never have wrung from him to the advantage of his assassin.

This essential clue consisted in the recognition of the hag of Illyria and the beautiful Vergilia as one and the same person. Now Janko had been her kinsman, and her intimate in her former existence, and had been privy and assistant (as we know) to the rite by which her youth was to be renewed. To him the inheritance was destined of the seal which she had constructed for this end, and by the existence of which alone her rejuvenescence could be effected. Upon the success of her experiment, after seven days of seeming death, it was intended that he should restore it to her; but we are already aware that, through the interference of the Venetian, that success he had never seen. The memory of his obligation being destroyed by the drug of the poisoner, the talisman that was bound up with it became the plaything of the bravo.

The plaything of the bravo we repeat, and it could never be anything else to him, so long as he remained in ignorance of the peculiar power it exerted over the transfigurated witch. For the amulet was the invisible load-stone that at the moment when first they met had drawn her head down irresistibly to his breast, where it lay concealed. Hold out as she might, she must nevertheless infallibly have ultimately yielded to the spell by which the Seven Sigils gave its holder power over her life. And Tosca had unwittingly exchanged it for Dead Sea fruit. The fantastical personage calling himself Magloire was, on the other hand, well aware (for reasons which, for the moment, we leave in the dark) of the power of the pawn he thus obtained.

His proffer of the bond, in the first instance, was a ruse (for he knew it would not be signed), and it served very well its end of diverting suspicion from his real purpose by making that appear an afterthought. Now that he had obtained the long-sought-for prize, he stopped in his work of demolishing his geometry (the bravo being no longer in sight), and stood for a long time collecting in the jewel every possible ray of light. Then he did a most extraordinary thing, even for him, whose every deed was extraordinary. He took it off its chain, which he threw carelessly away, and conveying the glittering heptagon to his mouth, he swallowed it.

There was method in his apparent madness. Its virtues would not suffer in the slightest from its imprisonment. The fortunes borne by its Seven Sigils for good or for evil were henceforth indissolubly bound up with his being. In this way he avoided any possible chance of its ever passing out of his possession. But the most urgent reason for his caution was the imminent return of his late assistant. He had gauged the character of that individual too deeply to feel safe while in his company.

And in his company, he evidently intended to remain. The sun had now risen, and the structure he had wrought by a word out of nothing was at last entirely visible. And he saw that it was good. The waters around it swarmed with love and feud between fishes, gold and silver and white aquatic birds. Other feathered life hopped the countless little streamers which adorned the shining turrets. A broad landing stage fronted the chief gate which was the higher of it to the extent of a magnificent flight of steps. As to the interior the Moorish lattices were inscrutable.

But curiosity need not long remain unsatisfied. The handsome pair for whom this casket was destined were already joyously approaching. The bravo started when he came in sight of the secretive Gaul still masked, and as at the moment when he left him rubbing out the traces of his circles. Vergilia started, as if in recognition of some acquaintance perchance of her youth. The vaguely mysterious Seven Sigils had launched their erotic work. The bravo surprised the attention which the Frenchman had excited—remembered that he had never liked him from the first—and began to look upon him as a possible rival.

But the desire to take French leave of him begot the bewildering discovery that although the castle floated, complete as per contract, he was powerless himself by any exertion of wish or will to cause it to sail to shore that they might enter in according to the original plan sketched out by its fair young architect. In this dilemma the Gaul came bowing and scraping to his aid, and showed that by a simple signal of his hand he could attract it to him as a magnet attracts iron. And now Tosca began to suspect the lurking of some design in all this. His suspicions were confirmed when Magloire stepped with them upon the threshold of their new home, and the palace immediately resumed its place in the centre of the Bottomless Lake.

There was now no chance for it but to admit the unwelcome guest. Their feet were lost to the ankles in the carpet that covered the nakedness of that royal flight of stairs we have already alluded to. They passed into a banqueting hall of exquisite proportion, and sculpt with a fairy chisel. Through keyhole arches that overlooked a central court, the melodies of all kinds of singing birds were wafted contrapuntally across the strains of the equally invisible musicians inside the banqueting hall itself, while the sun-litten flashings of a fountain formed the organ point that threaded through the whole—so much as this the Venetian came, and saw, and enjoyed; but as to the laced and liveried semblances of life with which the banqueting hall was alive, they were semblances of death for all the service which the wish and will of Tosca sought to exact from them.

And here again the Frenchman came to his aid, and these *genii*, at his command, throbbed with obsequious ichor. Tables (in a second, magnificently clothed) groaned under the newest of foods and beakers filled at the central spring (fed from the waters of the Bottomless Lake) brimmed with the oldest of wines. Vergilia and Magloire appeared infused with perfect life, but to the bravo all was bitter in the mouth. He saw by the action of the *genii* of the place that the contract agreed to, and possibly only too literally carried out, had not been sufficiently comprehensive. The day had dawned, it is true, upon a tenement that eminently satisfied the caprices of Vergilia.

But the bravo was only in name its master and hers. The castle that mocked his efforts to move it came and went at the motion of his rival, the servants that were automata to Tosca were alive to the bidding of Magloire, and Vergilia had forsaken her old love and beamed only upon the new. Nay, she cast upon Magloire the self-same love light which had fired Tosca's blood in her defence when he snatched her from her ravishers, that never to be forgotten day when first they met. He had thought his valour saved her from a fortune worse than death, which now he feared would have affected her not at all. For he saw that all the signs of an apparently virgin love could rise up like phoenix from the ashes of a past one.

And he shuddered to think how often this process might have been repeated. Had all her lovers then enjoyed her perchance save Tosca alone? And yet all the more she sank in his estimation, the fuller swelled the tide of his desire. The long luxurious banquet was a torture to him with this death's head at his feast. His rage increased steadily with the jealousy it fed upon. The long-drawn courses were no sooner over than he seized upon some trifling pretext (we know not what) to leave Vergilia alone for a few moments while he drew his rival to that central court, whence perfumed zephyrs blew. The stranger still continued masked. To this Tosca first alluded laying his hand upon the hilt of that famous old sword of his.

"Unmask your face that I may know you."

"You shall know me too well ere long."

"Restore me that amulet unearned by your accursed jugglery."

"You will never see it again."

"Then let this sword of justice decide between us that has settled many a case for me before, and the Devil help his own! But first reveal to me your real style and title (and a fig for the assumed one that you go by), that I may learn with what enemy I have to deal that has cause to hunt me down as you have hunted me."

"You deal with the Resenter and Avenger of the murder of the Illyrian."

A shiver ran down the spine of the Venetian. Yet his blade nevertheless flashed from its sheath, and he motioned to the stranger to take up a position opposite to him. Magloire turned round for one second to do so, and in that second the sword of his faithless foe was plunged remorselessly through his back. The point protruded through his breast. The next instant the sword had been withdrawn, and the still unexplained Frenchman lay prone upon the ground by the self-same stratagem that had availed with the man of whom he styled himself avenger.

And this time also the Venetian took the trouble to assure himself of the death of his victim before returning his sword to its scabbard. That done, he proceeded next to ascertain the real identity of this mysterious being whom he had supposed to be one of his numerous enemies working out a long-delayed vendetta. With a clutch the mask was torn to ribbons, and with a shriek the bravest of the brave recoiled from the Mandrake it revealed; and, as the shrieker heard his shriek, he recognised its kind.

It was fellow to that one he had heard the day before from

the chamber of Vergilia, never deeming that he himself in turn would be frighted with the same basilisk face. But it frighted him (after all) with a difference. The soul of the pot valiant courtier had been reft from its silken frame, but the tempered ribs of the Man of War held fast their trust within. His brain whirled and steadied itself—his blood shot forth and back again—his eye grew dark and cleared.

On to his knees he sank, indeed, that never had bent to conquered (or unconquered) foe before, but that was the only abatement from his pride of place. That was his only homage to the escaped familiar of the sorceress' privacy, that grim guardian whose gorgon glimpse had yesterday sobered the drunkard and petrified the itching flesh of lust. And the situation brought its panacea. Ignorant still of the effect of the Seven Sigils, he fancied he had discovered now why the sorceress had favoured the Mandragorean watchman with the love glance once reserved for Tosca. It must be because that monster also had rendered service to her virtue as the bravo had rendered it before.

One question still remained unanswered. Had Vergilia herself never seen the face of this awful animated root? Or had she, by daily touch, kept up from the very first plucking of the plant, so grown up along with its progressing hideosity as to feel no inception of abhorrence? At any rate, his Mandrakeship was now placed finally *hors de boudoir*. And the bravo reflected that he laughs best who laughs the last. Take heed, though, Tosca, there rests one yet unslain till the day of final doom, in whose danger you still stand, and whose claws are creeping towards you from the dark places of the earth! Who sups with the Devil had need have a very long spoon.

But now there flashes like a sunbeam through the court the golden-haired vision of whose destiny he now hoped himself sole arbiter. Roused by that fell shriek, her anxiety nevertheless was far from being for the utterer of it. With a cry of agonised acute despair, she flung past the outstretched arms of the bravo on to the prostrate body of the lover still bound to her in death by the magic of the talisman he had swallowed with so justified a foresight. The bravo knelt no longer to the Mandrake, but to her, and with a cry plucked up the thoughts of his deepest soul.

"Thou wanton and thing of many lovers, yet whom still I madly love! By the love you once bore me, have pity on me now and vouchsafe me but the leavings of this man or monster. A living dog is better than a dead lion, so they say. Call me your dog or what you will, so that you call me yours. For you I placed my soul in pledge, and would you now desert me in my indignity? Nay then, if your choice be irrevocably riveted to this carrion, so be it! But you shall share the fate of him whom you so fancy. The *Grand Seignieur* is connoisseur in the art of fittest punishing the faithless. With my own eyes I have seen his favourite odalisques sewn up in sacks, and dropped into the Bosphorus. And with my own hands I will deal with you even so. You shall have your fill of local colour ere you have done with your palace of the East."

The bravo was now crouching instead of kneeling, and gathering himself up into a spring as of a panther he plunged upon the still disconsolable mourner. Twining his fingers recklessly about the golden hair he oft had kissed, he dragged her, not without difficulty from the corpse of the Thing, whose fall she wept, jerking her spasmodically into the hall and overturning its furniture right and left. Amid the crashing of shattered bric-a-brac, he grabbed at the nearest cushion from a divan that stood hard by, and ripping out its entrails with the ferocity of an attack upon a living thing, he felled the shrieking girl to the ground with a blow that would have startled an ox, and forced his contrived receptacle somehow and anyhow over her body, she uttering never a syllable the while.

Did she think that he had no heart to carry to a finish such a deed? Or was it still the eccentric influence of the Seven Sigils that made death to her preferable to life apart from the one beloved? This we cannot answer. Enough that Tosca seemed in deadly earnest as he shook together the members of his mistress, and compressing the mouth of his improvised sarcophagus, tied it up with the belt from his waist. This done he left it on the couch, and returned to the central court drowsy with incense laden flowers. He intended to yield Vergilia one more chance.

Left to herself, and already wrapped in her winding sheet, the present expectation of a painful death would surely lead to second thoughts, and induce her to lavish less carelessly the future of her youth and beauty—the splash that heralded the committal of her paramour to the water would be echoed by her appeal for mercy—and he had resolved in that case to forgive her the worst she dared confess to him. But now to the work. Not entirely without spasms of fresh fear he re-entered the courtyard of the fateful duel, and where the duellist who had fallen lay. His body the bravo now conveyed down the steps to the landing stage in front of the main building.

It did not fail to occur to the practical mind of the Venetian as he strained under the repulsive corpse of his quondam adversary that somewhere upon his person (as he thought) must lie concealed the talisman of the Seven Sigils. He did not know that to find it he should have to search for it within and not without. The consequence naturally was that his search was unrewarded by any trace whatever of the coveted gem. But the more he searched and pondered—and pondered and searched again—the more he became convinced of the necessity for finding it, and the clearer became to him the momentous part it had played in recent events.

He remembered now too late that while he had it in his possession his suit with Vergilia had prospered, whereas Heaven had begun to frown upon him as soon as he had parted with it to Magloire. He was too shrewd a conjuror to fail to connect the one fact with the other, and with them both the anxiety of the Mandrake to possess the talisman of whose virtues he had obviously knowledge. Yet still it could not be found upon his person. With a fearful oath the Venetian at length gave up the search, and consigned the fruitless body to the Bottomless Lake. He would find the bauble yet (he swore) by all his left hand gods in whatsoever nook of earth it lay.

And with that very oath upon his lips he cast it off unwittingly for ever, deep buried in the body that he spurned. Flotsam and jetsam whatsoever touched the surface of those Stygian waves became the forfeit of the Fiend. Such was the fate of body and gem. No more to appear in substance in our story, the seal of the Seven Sigils shall, nevertheless, ride through it to the end, completing the curse of the Illyrian. The Venetian (ignorant as we have said of the loss, he had inflicted upon himself) once more re-entered the banqueting hall. His purpose, before dealing with the question of his lady-love, was to order up a second! collation accompanied by fresh founts of wine. This *tête-à-tête* (as he ordained it in his mind) should obliterate the memory of the previous banquet with its presence of an inconvenient third.

He gave his order roundly to the servants, quite forgetting how impotent his commands. The automata remained unmoved, save for the fancy of the bravo that they leered somewhat upon him with an unmistakeable expression of contempt. Stung to sudden rage he drew his keen ancestral blade, and made a lunge at the vitals of the nearest one. In a moment he saw his mistake. The steel shivered into a thousand fragments, and shattered in its flight all the mirrors of the room. The hilt alone remained in his hand, which was jarred through and through by the shock. But the mental effect was even worse.

For the first time a sense of impending Nemesis began to steal upon him. This unique companion of all his vicissitudes had been beloved of his inmost soul. From his jeopardous early days up, he had been accustomed never to sleep without it, until it had become almost necessary to his slumbers that he should clap it to his breast. Slowly he recovered, and even comforted himself. What could his ancient hanger on avail him in his imprisonment on that island of enchantment? And had he not at hand metal far more attractive—damaskeened with gold—and suppler than Damascus steel? He gathered together lingeringly the shards of his faithful bedfellow, that he might cast those also into that Bottomless Lake that had just received their latest victim.

But when he had them all embraced together in his arms, and had thrown aside the portal that he might descend the steps to the landing stage—he was blasted with a shock not so easy to rebound from as this matter of a broken weapon—there existed no longer a landing stage at all! Where it formerly stood the remorseless tide of the Bottomless Lake now swept the foot of the steps! The bravo reeled. For a moment the air was thick with curses loud and deep upon the day when the Seven Sigils had first flashed its baleful light athwart his path.

He now saw the full significance of the fact that Magloire alone could shift the castle's site, and vivify its phlegmatic flunkeydom. The castle having been created by Magloire, for him alone existed. The handing over of his body to Beelzebub, of which the bravo himself had been the unthinking agent, had finally snapped the charm which held the building in existence. It was now slowly sinking into the waters from which it rose, and would continue to slowly sink till not a stone of it was visible above the surface of the darkling deep. Tosca reeled at this slap in the face that his fortune dealt him.

He never knew how he found himself once more within the central court, a beaker in his hand, filling it to the brim with a vintage of the fountains of which we made mention before. He raised the vessel to his lips. The next moment it fell from his palsied hand and dashed into a thousand pieces. The fluid he had tried to drink slobbered over his knees as he rolled ignominiously upon the tessellated pavement. It was no longer wine that the fountain had yielded, but the fetid water of the Bottomless Lake! And this also resulted from the breaking of the charm by burial of the body of Magloire.

The curse of the Illyrian was closing in upon its victim. The fate of the Venetian was written large upon his forehead. Abrupt despair gripped upon his heart-strings. Yet still the honour of the bout remained with Tosca. For he remembered in his extremity that the bundle on the couch with all its possibilities was his. In despite of all that doom had done he still remained the owner of a wallet that beggared Fortunatus. He sprang to his feet like an Antaeus, all the tenser for his momentary lapse to earth. He stretched out his arms towards the Bottomless Lake, and roared in tones of thunder:—

"Hell from beneath is moved for me to meet me at my coming! Now runs my sand apace, and I am ripe for my enrolment in the legions that eternally curse God and do not die! Yet still the victory of victories is mine, and eyeless Death shall not outstare me from it! Is it for this you work (you who sit in the High Places of the Pit), that I should flaunt in your faces the most fragrant hour of Life? Oh, how you have wrought your work awry! And you—you myriad victims of the dagger or the bowl that I have ushered unannealed to the account—I invite you every one to my bridal! Is this then your vengeance (oh, viperine Magloire!) that fruition should wait on my desire?

"And you, Illyrian Janko, is this then your revenge that you watch my wedding eve from the impotent other side of that great gulf fixed between? Here, on this side, I exact value in advance for the eternal price I pay. Here shall our ardent heat outblaze your fires, and when your ruffian waters reach our level shall the floor above receive us—and still the floor above—till on the roof itself at last we still out-laugh you! Hours must elapse or ever your icy billows reach our hearts, and wash them to the portal of Infinity! These hours shall be mine (though all Gehenna gnash its teeth), and our content shall give the lie to Hell"

Firm as a rock, he strode to his bag and cast off the belt from its mouth. A head appeared. But not a golden one. Its scanty hair was grey. Tosca recoiled. The ground reeled beneath him. His brain was furnace, and his blood arterial snow. With a mighty effort he recovered himself, and leaped like a madman into the sack, rending it seam from seam. The whole fabric parted, and disclosed, not the nonpareil that he had placed in its safe keeping, but the withered stubs of limbs and yellow disjected trunk of that ancient harridan of Illyria, whom he had seen on that never to be forgotten former occasion anatomised by the hand of Janko. And as he stared dead eyed upon that death, he was mercifully unaware that his feet were being swept by the inexorable waves of the advancing Bottomless Lake.

The Hand of Glory

PART 1

MINE HOST OF THE FOUR CROSS ROADS

The year of grace 1609. Our scene, a tavern within, and yet apart from, the bustle of a seaport town. Damned by its site upon an ill-omened juncture of crossroads, which, at a time when the town had not straggled so far, had been the burial ground of suicide and sorcerer: haunted by bones still sleepless, although centuries had gone since their last rag of flesh reeked off into the medicinal air; solitary in a crowd, except for such strangers as never learnt the local traditions. For these very reasons it attracted the attention of a class that feared men more than ghosts; and thus, it came to be whispered among the neighbours as the house of call for the wizards of the Basque Provinces.

Such was the situation upon which the curtain rises. Our readers may now form a guess as to the character of the traveller that sought admittance upon the evening in question. This traveller was apparently alone—only apparently—for another sentient being suddenly makes known to us his presence on the scene. The cabalistic ring which graced the finger of our traveller shot a double-lightning from its tenant stone as the fist of its lord beat a devil's tattoo on the tavern door. The demon that was imprisoned within the ring had lifted for one second his pendulous eyelids.

Foreknowledge of his approaching freedom to be wrought under that roof (as this chronicle shall in due order tell), had touched up buried fires; but patience born of immortality resumed its pride of place, and the Demon dissembling again a hope too soon revealed, there died in the instant all light from the gem, and left it fuscous as before. The fist in knocking was naturally raised above the head of the cabalist that wore the ring. The traveller consequently failed to perceive the eyebeams of his familiar. Be sure if he caught sight of that glint of evil glee, he would have read in it an omen of impending disaster to the enterprise that turned him to that tavern. The future of cabalist and demon would then have hung upon his decision whether to dree the weird or 'scape it.

But the significants that ruled his horoscope withheld the timely warning, and the traveller continued his endeavours to get hearing from the all too early retired household. Thus, the moment of possible retreat passed irrevocably by. A wicket sunk in the stubborn thickness of the door, was thrown suddenly open. A pair of eyes appeared—luminous, terrible. They fixed those of the cabalist unflinchingly, beams to beams, lights to lights, and the cabalist recognised in the eyes of his adversary the self-same, tell-tale film through which he flashed his own.

Not the film of the eagle neither, that may enable the king of birds to peruse the noonday sun, but would impotently shrivel before the venomous exhalations that stream from fiery pits that blaze under fallen angels' brows, no, the eyes of the intervisible twain were sheathed with the shard of the born exorcist—the heir of the secrets and physical gifts of a line of wizard sires. From behind these horny casements they had measured the frown of Satan's self, and danced undaunted and undulled; Sparse were the mortals whom the cabalist reckoned fellow-men; but here, at any rate, was one of them. The cabalist waxed kindly, as he proceeded to interrogate what he felt to be a kindred spirit.

"Is this the hostelry of the Four Cross Roads?"

"By some such name is it noted among the vulgar."

"And are you he of whom they whisper, under the name of Aquelarre?"

"I am the master of this house."

"You are then he to whom I am recommended by one I have good reason to trust."

"May I trouble you for his name?"

"To me he is known as Lisaldo."

"Under that name, at any rate, I do not know him; but that argues nothing. A thousand soldiers know the lieutenant whom the lieutenant does not know."

"By this token you may know him, that he gave you a name of praise and fear—that of the devil's correspondent for the viscounty of Labourt."

"And if it were so?"

"Then over and above being yourself sunk from sole to crown in the study of supernature you have, traced the gigantic plan of linking yourself together with all else that tread untrodden ways. And I saw that the design was good—for in union there is strength—and if we in the far New World from which I come, are today unthreatened by the bigotry of the church, it would nevertheless be short sight indeed if we played the spectator, while among you runs the writ of cord and faggot. Tomorrow, mayhap, we shall be persecuted in our turn, and ashes the brethren that could have bettered us.

"For this, then, am I travelled hither, as I may say at your bidding, since the suggestion proceeded from one who knows you, though him you may not know; that we may survey together the field of your danger, and in consort draft such measure of defiance and defence as shall eat up this persecution at the root. This evening disembarked and understanding from that same Lisaldo, that under cover of the tavern of the Four Cross Roads your pursue your devil's procuracy, I have hustled hither straight to take up my quarters beneath your kindly roof."

"Are you then alone or do I rightly see two others that linger in your rear among the shadows?"

"The one of them is this Lisaldo that I speak of, to whom I owe your name, and who has attached himself to my personal service; and in this connexion I may mention that I shall require two communicating bedrooms (or be it one with a dressing-room adjacent) to gratify my long, and now invincible, vogue of keeping my servant all night within my call. My other follower is a *creole* of the family Ataurresagasti; by trade an honest seaman, but not, I believe, too honest to be of possible use to our cause. Told off to do us service during the long and perilous passage he has been only too anxious to be of comfort to us, and we are indebted to him for countless little offices.

"Arrived at your wharves we could satisfy him with nothing less than the porterage of half our effects, and since the whole were too heavy for Lisaldo, 'twas but policy to accept his friendly offer, rather than initiate a stranger into our destination. Accommodated with a bed in this same house, he will be under our united ken—should you consider him metal that may be moulded to our purpose he need never return to his ship"

"Nor for the matter of that in the contrary case either, since it were unsafe for him to have even touched the skirts of our common secret. 'Tis child's play for such as you and I to rot the thread of life with an oblivious gruel."

"We will confer upon that matter in the bedroom which you allot me, while Lisaldo and the sailor are refreshing themselves below. You are satisfied with my credentials, and will admit us without delay, since the night is wasting shrewdly?"

"There is one thing wanting—your name."

"My name I have never syllabled since my birth, nor would it be possible to deceive you with a false one, you being what you are and I wearing this ring by whose fame you and all of life occult may know me."

The cabalist jerked his slender hand from out of the folds of his cloak, where he had thrust it after the opening of the wicket. Its crouching prisoner (wiser than before) allowed never a wink to escape him. But that it was in sooth the very ring that contained the familiar (renowned among the sorcerers of the whole round world) Aquelarre well could see. An insane impulse to strike down the insolent owner, and incontinently seize the matchless gem, contracted every fibre of his body. Had the door not stood; between them, he would have made the rash attempt, only to remember, when too late, that the allegiance of the Demon could never by violence transfer from man to man.

He ground the wicket into its place to hide the distortion of his features, and busied himself with bolts and bars that they might clatter above the gnashing of his teeth. By the time he had undone the fastenings the impulse had passed. Recollecting all the restrictions that fenced the ring around, he had become once more himself. Meanwhile the nameless cabalist had summoned with a whistle his two attendants forward. Youths of about an equal age, the one was white as a cosset page, and the other tanned like a galley-slave.

The massive portal swung a-side with a suddenness that even drew a start from the seasoned nerves of the cabalist, though it must be evident that one who had put together such a ring must be steeped in no ordinary course of sciences and surprises. A blaze of light shot through the widening passage into the dark deserted street. A host of obsequious hands stretched out of the blinding drift and relieved the two bearers of their luggage. Before the three newcomers had acquired the proper focus to even perceive who had thus helped them, the helpers were out of sight.

Viands and vintages which had appeared with startling rapidity alone remained to prove to their eyes which the travellers rubbed, the substantiality of the just present bodies. Also, the master of the house stood there, unbonneted, and bowing his welcome. The cabalist refused to break a fast which was integral to some experiment in hand; leaving this, then, to the more congenial age of Lisaldo and the sailor, he withdrew with Aquelarre to his apartments. Thus, the youths so like, and yet so unlike, at last were left alone together.

The footfalls of the brothers of the black art had hardly died away above stairs when the sailor turned to Lisaldo abruptly and whispered in a tone attuned to every sweetness—

"Lisalda!"

The page started as if stung to death, at thus hearing an address in the feminine form of the name, instead of in the masculine. His face at first blanched with sudden terror, and then flooded with rosy red. He made a confused attempt at correction.

"You mean Lisaldo."

"Lisalda, and Lisalda, and Lisalda."

The sailor persisted—this apparent error seemed to water in his mouth—then remembering himself he became sheepish as a chidden child, and sank presently on to his knees. The page eyed him guiltily, then the sailor took courage in his hands and made sensible his inmost heart.

"I love you, Lisalda, and love has keener sight than many that call it blind. I felt your sex from the first hour you stepped aboard. I kindled to it with an instinct that strangled reason. It possessed every fibre of me through all our days becalmed on Sargasso seas that to me seemed flower shotten meads. I clenched my teeth on it our tropic nights when hand in hand you walked my watch with me, and learnt from me the blazonry of heaven. Months ago, I should have given throat to the heart that hungered within me. But in my surly sailor fashion I only tightened my belt around it. I am no saint, Lisalda, I have served apprentice to buccaneers on Caribbean seas—men that never set a hand to honest tool save when they planted chests of gold in the earth, I have swam o' days in blood and o' nights in wine.

"But the hand that scattered the brains of Don and Dutchman was an aspen held in yours. Terror tremendously overruled me, when I would fain have slipped the cable of my desire, and it is a marvel to me now that I kneel at your feet, though I know full well that my revealment is wrung from me by the parting asunder of our ways. Here must I speak or ever after hold my peace, here you may infuse yourself with a heart no less honest than rough, that has beat for naught nor will beat for aught save you; or here you may rule me unworthy of more that has already enjoyed overmuch. It bodes me ill I fear, Lisalda, that you never read a heart so confounded with your own; but whatever you say will be for me the voice of oracle that is worshipped whether good or ill."

"The oracle is dumb tonight, Ataurresagasti, though you have taught me that I knew your love from the first. I cannot decide at once whether I have done you irreparable wrong, or added to your fulness of life. Tomorrow, friend (if that title does not jar upon you) shall learn you all your heart's desire. And (whatever that morrow's disillusion) tonight at any rate, your image will disturb my no longer virgin sleep."

"Your sleep, Lisalda, there's the rub that galls my jealous loin. Tonight, that I have a share in you (though it be but for tonight) I shudder at the thought of your retiring to the ante-room of the bedchamber of that other man. Throughout the voyage every lip before the mast has shriven him with curses (not loud, but deep) for the wayward winds his Jonah presence fetched athwart our course. The bated breath of the forecastle credited him with the wearing of a familiar spirit imprisoned in the setting of that ring upon his hand. How did such as you come to foregather with one so unkindly, and withal so far from this your birthplace? And what is his need of you that one so powerful should claim you close at heel?"

"Ataurresagasti, it were too long to tell you how I came to be orphaned, and at buffet with the world. Too long again to recount the chances that transferred me from here to the Indies. Enough that I must have been in desperate straits when I donned the disguise I still wear, and entered the vacant service of my present lord and master. That he lived in evil odour had come to my ears, and that he never kept his servants long, but that they either went mad or died was more than gossip to me that first attended my master to the funeral of my predecessor. I was situated so sorely that I would have worn Satan's livery to earn me bed and board.

"Now the secret of the wants of my master and the wastage amongst his servants is this: his nerves are completely shattered by terrible experiments, the nature of which I never dare to know. He sees through the veil that round us wraps impenetrably. He is haunted day and night by hosts of beings incorporate awful. Over these, indeed, some sway of his extends (else were he long since torn to shreds), but only by the continual strain of every resource of his science.

"The demon that is familiar of the ring you speak of—the loathsome creepiness that writhes within a crystal cell and impotently spits at such as dare to see—is on the one hand the crowning glory of his labours, and the envy of the wizard world—and on the other hand an anxious horror that makes cheap the mere routine of Hell. Day it turns to night, night to nightmare, and still the worst of all remains—the hour between midnight and cockcrow when the heavenly patrols are relieving guard and the nether gates swing open and all the rout of Hell are free to seek their own devilish devices. Now you can guess, can you not, Ataurresagasti, why the cabalist never remains alone in the dark?"

"By the God I never praised till I met you, Lisalda, this passes the worst I had imagined. But do you still think so ill of me (after the centuries of mingled life we have crushed into so curt an orbit), do you still so little value my self-esteem as to believe me capable (now I know what your service is) of allowing you to continue it for even yet one grain of the hour glass? To the devil with this enemy and friend of his, and let the poor prisoner of the ring have his day! I, too, am a prisoner and feel for all in bonds."

"You are the best of men, Ataurresagasti, and fittest to be free. But for this night at any rate (however your reasons may touch me) I must fulfil my contract, as of use and wont. Whatever new combination tomorrow's sun may bring, it is too late tonight, at any rate, to find a substitute to comrade the broken slumbers of the cabalist."

"It is never too late, Lisalda, to crown my broad shoulders with the lightness of a burden saved from yours. I beseech you, as a lover whom, you may yet reject, not to refuse me this (as it may be) last sad privilege—chance itself (if all be not fated from the first) plays patron to my innocent stratagem. The landlord of this tavern of the Four Cross Roads (and may I die the day I see a more ill-favoured fellow) has heard our names, it is true, but can have no means of telling which is which.

"Do you call yourself the cabin-boy, Ataurresagasti, and vouchsafe me for one brief snatch, to be bone of the bone, and flesh of the flesh with Lisalda (or Lisaldo). The certainty that you are bolted and barred once more in a room alone, will bear me up through all that teems from Tophet. The cabalist is the only eye that could detect the substitution, and he keeps (or you would never have remained his) respectfully on his own side the partition until morning. The dawn may see him damned, so far as his hold on either of us is concerned, and we will set forth (together I trust) about our own peace and pleasure."

"As to that I can give you no promise, Ataurresagasti, save to remember you in any case until the last sigh of life. But this, as you say, is all the more reason why I should let you be my proxy, if it will give you any unfeigned satisfaction. And here comes back our host on the heels of our accord, and the curtain rises on our play."

The sailor rose to his feet. It was as Lisalda said, for such (her secret once revealed) we may as well henceforth style her, Aquelarre having finished his business with the cabalist come to summon the page to his attendance. But he first drew a bottle and three goblets from a press and placed the latter on one of the tables. Filling them to the overflow, he appointed one to each to drink a parting cup. All three raised on high and touched together their goblets in token of sentiment, somewhat hollow. Ataurresagasti had scarcely put his lips to the liquid, when memory started armed from his brain. It was hocussed. There was no doubt about it. He had been drugged once before by the press-gang of the pirate, with whom he had served out his buccaneer articles.

Once bit, twice shy. He replaced the goblet on the table, the other two mechanically followed his example. The good fellowship that shone upon his weather-beaten face was in inverse ratio to the ready subtlety that scanned every loophole from within; and presently he swooped down with unerring instinct upon the only possible coign of vantage. The meaning eyes of the landlord had turned upon the innocent eyes of Lisalda. He was staring out her inmost soul. Taking advantage of this absorption of the two, Ataurresagasti reversed the positions of the drugged goblet and that of the landlord.

So smartly did he execute this manoeuvre that it would most certainly have escaped the notice of an ordinary observer. But had it escaped the lynx-eyed Aquelarre? The sailor breathed more freely when, upon all three once more raising their goblets, the whole of the hocussed stuff disappeared without question down the landlord's corded throat. All having drained to the dregs, Aquelarre turned and addressed himself to the quondam buccaneer:—

"May I be burnt by the Parliament of Bordeaux if my customer upstairs let me into the secret as to which of you two, he mastered. Now I'll be bound 'tis you, my jolly Roger (and not this queasy cabinboy) that has chaffered for gold his rest o' nights to the wandering Jew up aloft there."

"Your guess does honour to your penetration, Monsieur Four Cross Roads, though you did overshoot your bolt a bit when you called me Jolly Roger."

"Ho, ho. Monsieur Lisaldo, so you turned your skin then with your livery, and no longer acknowledge the Black Flag?"

"How do you know that I had ever anything in common with the Black Flag?"

"Easy as lying, Monsieur Lisaldo, easy as lying. Your face, my friend (and for the matter of that, everyone's face), is as an open book whereon I read. Nay, your hand alone, my friend, shouts your past, your present, and your future to such as I that have ears to hear."

"Of the past and of the present I am already sick at heart, but I am open to receive any index (what it may befit me to know) as to how the future shall shape itself before me."

"A good wish upon you! I am permitted to tell you, at any rate, that you chose your vocation under a healthy star, for you were never born to be drowned!"

The sailor hardly knew whether to be amused or annoyed at the tone adopted by the chiromantist. He continued to balance the matter in a confused sort of way, after he had taken shy leave of Lisalda. Arrived in his room, he barred and bolted the outer door with a thoroughness born of much adventuring. He loosened a hanger that he wore at his side, and tied it by its belt as with a sword knot to his wrist. That had been the *toilet de rigueur* for the night among his former messmates, the pirates of the Antilles.

In this array then, supine upon the bed, he confidently awaited developments. To keep himself awake he continued to agitate the mysterious character and conduct of Aquelarre. The events of the evening, since the ill-assorted three had left their ship together, all forced themselves into the question.

This opened the road to a review of the whole voyage and the change it had wrought in his life. And that life—what turn would it take on the morrow? What result from the heart-probing of Lisalda? The singularity was that the more plausible he painted the future, the darker shaded the present, and the past, of his sweetheart. He felt it was an insult to her to question her about that past of which she had denied the recital. And yet he longed—and how he longed—to rise to her from his very bed to question her. And her relations with the cabalist—how long before the voyage she had served him Ataurresagasti never knew, but apart from that it was gall and wormwood to him that she should even have shared his state room at sea.

The fancy forced itself upon the sailor that the cabalist—who saw through all things—had seen through her disguise. The more he turned over the reasons assigned by Lisalda for the cabalist never sleeping alone, the more unlikely it appeared that a prince of all the Magi, and tamer of the Demon of the Ring, should show a side so puny. In spite of his better self, there forced itself upon him another, and quite opposite, picture of the nights that these two had passed together. Yet why (and here for a moment he threw off that thraldom) yet why had Lisalda, this particular evening, apparently willingly exchanged with him the place, which by that hateful theory she should have found a pleasance. Again, wider issues loomed in every direction, until he returned again bewildered to what seemed willy-nilly his keynote for that night. He tossed from side to side.

Picture after picture stood out before his mind's eye, until he even reached the length of fancying Lisalda at that moment on the other side with the cabalist, while Ataurresagasti on his side lay befooled. That she could not have got there by any human means was a difficulty which did not even occur to him for solution. The sweat stood out thick upon his brow. He positively saw Lisalda twined about the body of his rival. His hair (he felt it) was turning grey. He saw the cabalist (a wonder of satiety) remove that ring of rings from his finger and fit it jestingly upon hers.

At this precise juncture of his nightmare, Ataurresagasti suddenly started broad awake to his feet. Dream or no dream—whatever the rest of the night had been—there was certainly now something awful in progress in the adjoining apartment.

Something (which he instinctively felt was not human) was struggling for life and death with the luckless cabalist. The hair of the sailor stood on end. There was no mistake about it this time. Time had been when he fancied he felt fear, but he knew now that only at this moment had he learnt its kind. All at once a most terrible shriek rang out through every corner of the house. Ataurresagasti dashed the partition into splinters with a blow that would have shattered steel. He leaped into the room just in time to arrest the escape of some huge incredible beast, that stood sullenly at bay, in the straggling streak of dawn.

The mystery was solved. Down came the hanger with an impulse so irresistible that it sheared off a whole limb of the accursed one. The point of the hanger actually penetrated so deeply into the flooring that it was a moment of anxiety (during which his quarry, although maimed, might have bested him) before Ataurresagasti succeeded in getting it out again. But when he had recovered it, the animal had disappeared, impossible to find out how or where. This alone he saw in the imperfect light (or rather in the imperfect darkness) that the whole room was scattered from end to end with bipod and bones and brain, which was all that was left of that most unhappy man.

A sickness came upon the victor. He mopped his dripping forehead. He turned to leave the presence-chamber of death and doom; he picked up as he did so the severed limb, a casual glance at which confirmed his general impression that the gaunt game had been but a particularly large and loathly wolf, such as occasionally penetrated the precincts of towns in the neighbourhood of the Pyrenees. Ataurresagasti walked down straight into the reception room of the night before. For the moment the possible alarm of Lisalda at that terrible shriek of dissolution of the cabalist had not even entered his mind. His object was to summon Aquelarre. To his surprise he found him crouching there already white as a ghost apparently with fear.

He sprang to his feet at sight of the sailor, and barely suppressed a cry. This time it was the sailor that read, and the landlord's face that provided reading matter. Amazement was writ legibly in, every line of it, and his eyes were opened to the size of saucers. And Ataurresagasti asked himself, without finding answer, what connexion all this had with the attempt to drug him, which he had discovered the preceding evening. The two men stared at one another for some minutes without finding speech, of which indeed the innkeeper, at any rate, seemed incapable. The word when taken up was taken up by Ataurresagasti.

"My pharmaceutical friend seems somewhat upset by my early appearance after draining the drowsy cup which he compounded for me overnight."

"And it is not natural that a landlord should be fearful for his slate when he sees an uncancelled score slinking downstairs to the outlet at such unearthly hour?"

"Alas, for your slate (if that touch you so nearly) a fiscal fleeter than yourself has attended here this night, and collected your other lodger's scot."

"What means this Matin pleasantry? How goes it with, the cabalist?"

"Well, I hope, although I dare not think it well. His reckoning, I fear, will overreach him."

"Is he dead?"

"As much of him as can still be traced is unquestionably dead."

"That then undid my beauty sleep. I thought I dreamed an unforgetful shriek."

"'Twas murder mouthed it. God rest his soul, that died in such a case as he was overtaken in."

"He died, you say, by the hand of God?"

"I say by the limb of a wolf, rather, which I arriving overdue did incontinently lop from its trunk. The felon then evading by exit to me invisible, I descended hither by what impulse I scarcely know save that my intentions tended justiceward."

"You meant perchance to summon authority to certify to cause of death. But this must be looked to by myself before anyone else is admitted. What became of the piece of conviction?"

"Behold it!"

"Out upon you! What providence have we here! O perjured windpipe you are most miraculously self-accused by this mischosen joint! Limb of a wolf did you dare to say? Nay, behold assassin, to your confusion, 'tis the disjointed member of your master that you have brought away with you from the presence chamber."

A cry of horror burst from the palsied lips of the sailor. It was as Aquelarre stated. Not the hacked-off trophy of his prowess had he carried in his hand; by some inexplicable equivocation it was the sundered fist of the cabalist still bearing the ring of the familiar. Chilled to the marrow by the ghastly riddle Ataurresagasti stammered some broken phrase of explanation; but the landlord cut him short.

"Hold your peace, rogue (and fool as much as rogue), you have miscast your account if you think to cope in a game of brag with a man of the world like Aquelarre. You do but squander breath which you may want ere long when the hangman ties your cravat. 'Twas then the bauble on yonder finger whose fatuous fire lured you into slippery sin—I misfancied even yesternight your gallows visage, that will ere long grin through a halter: 'twill clog my conscience till the day I die that I whispered no warning to that gentle sage. But by these five bones! I will lay no second blood to my debit. Rather than see a gallant (if misguided) boy turn rope-dancer I will hold the nose of correction from your trail. But think not that I shall also permit you to lay that flattering booty to your soul—you must make over to me the gaud that cozened you to crime.

"Indeed, if I left it in your possession, you would never dare to look a clothesline in the face. Whereas, never doubt but that I shall make the best possible use of it, such as I have no time to bethink myself of at the moment. Masses (perchance) for the soul of its late owner done to death unofficed by Holy Church. Whatever he would have liked to do for me had I been slain, and he Aquelarre. Oh, I can promise you a binding promise of that. But we palter out the time of opportunity. Your safety lies in instant flight. The Bidassoa lies within easy avail. Take the bridge that throws over it at Behobia. Once on the Spanish side of the river, the hemp is not sown that shall throttle you. For this crime at any rate, I remaining shall run the risk, if risk there be to run. Quick then with the gewgaw—'tis a dull stone at best—why do you hesitate when the path divides before you? One way leads to length of life, the other is a short cut to cordage."

"You son of a burnt witch! The broom-ridden hag that taught you to spell out the Devil's books, and to find fortunes in hands—past, present, and future forsooth—she taught you all askew. I have done no such deeds as your second sight credits me with. The matter squared precisely with my account of it, but I am fortune's fool, and in change for my own handiwork I took hold (I know not how) of this Hand of Glory. In view of the public opinion that whispers you a wizard I should not exclaim over and above if it turned out to be your own *hocus pocus* that brought about the barter.

"Nay, it is possible and even probable that the wolf was but a go-between, guided by a hand not a hundred miles from here (and I spit upon mine that grasped it in friendship yester-even) but you are seemingly only an understrapper in the Devil's workshop since you cut only yourself with your unnecessary tool. We did not do these things by deputy upon the Spanish Main. Viewed in the light of your press for the possession of the ring (of whose virtues you apparently believe me to be ignorant) the riddle of last night's sleeping draught need not long remain unread. That after stripping you to this nakedness I should clothe you with the purple and fine linen of the ring would be too much for any but yourself to expect."

"Cry you mercy! You have signed your own death-warrant. What you cast in my teeth is guesswork. But you are rivetted hand and foot to the matter of fact. Pass me the ring and you go free—refuse, and you shall play the pendulum."

"And would you play the gatesman? Odds my life, and do you think I dare not go free until Aquelarre lifts the latch? Deputy devil, look to yourself!"

Aquelarre placed his back to the door. The buccaneer swooped down upon him with a yell that split the throat of echo. With all his force he struck him in the face with the abominable relic of the cabalist. The effect was electric. Aquelarre threw up his arms, and fell like a log dumb and blind to the ground. The buccaneer wrenched open the door and disappeared down one of the Four Cross Roads.

PART 2

THE DEVIL'S ATTORNEY

The dial had sweat twelve hours of day ere we resume the broken thread of our story. At the sign of the Four Cross Roads (whether accident or design) matters stood in some such case as when we opened our first part. The cabalist having paid the debt which he had owed so lightly and so long, the ring now graced the little finger of the sailor. The inscrutable door strained under his muscular fist, that this time summoned passage. It opened, and again, with startling abruptness, Ataurresagasti crossed the fateful lintel. The door (which apparently worked of itself) flew back with a horrid, ominous jar. Aquelarre stood with his arms crossed in an attitude of expectation. Sailor and sorcerer took stock of one another from head to foot. But when the latter caught sight of the ring, he burst (as if inspired) into speech.

"So, you have returned upon your tracks; I foresaw you would, and have awaited you. You remembered, when in safety yonder side of the frontier, that you had left a jewel in danger behind, outweighing that you wear. Desire came uppermost in the throw with fear."

"You man of second sight, is she still here—since you know it is a she I seek?"

"You set me a painful task (my friend and admirer), if you are so ignorant of all that has happened during your somewhat protracted constitutional as to require the rigmarole of it from me. However, since you already doubtless know (and at any rate I care not to conceal from you) that I am the official representative in Labourt of a certain proud and damned prince, you doubtless look to me as to the fountain head. So be it then, and to the task. But you did a black day's work as ever you did under the Black Flag, when you saved your hide this morning at the expense of your mistress's skin. Nay, hear me out. I know that you were shaken out of all self.

"But you had scarcely kicked my dust from off your feet, when the officers of justice, whom you so churlishly evaded had plucked me by the beard. The swan song of him from whom you filched that ring had pierced the universal ear. That murder had deflowered the bed you wot of, the constables had no room to doubt. Indeed, your Carib fashion of piecemealing a victim put them to the unsavoury task of making out an inventory of the deceased. My own good fame being above suspicion, it fell from the first upon Lisalda, unearthed and laid willy-nilly by the heels. Her sex (another item of distrust about her) was of necessity discovered in the Torture Chamber."

"The Torture Chamber!"

"Aye, the Torture Chamber. You saved your four limbs. She will never use again one of her arms, that was crippled in their grips of hellish engines. The surgeon (save the mark) pronounced that she could bear no more today. Tomorrow they practice upon the other arm. And after that there will be enough of her sweet body to feed their tools a week."

"But she is innocent—my God, how innocent—and I, who begin almost to believe that I am guilty, will surrender at once in her place."

"Small good (my untutored friend), save the melancholy satisfaction of pressing the same rack with her. The Parliament of Bordeaux never let slip a single victim, nor is it any longer merely the indictment for the murder of the Cabalist that piles the faggots for her. You are a babe and suckling in these horrors. I am prematurely grey with them. Had you but seen (as I have) the mother burnt with the child at her breast—the loving pair chilled at the same stake—the friendship of years dissolved in smoke, but enough—to get out of the Torture Chamber (as you should readily guess) the *corpus vile* reduced to a crushed craze will sign any depositions that may be held out as a bait.

"The consequence is that your girl has already avowed her identity with a desperate, long-sought-for witch and sacristan to one of the most noted of our Black Priests. So much for the wringing of one set of nerves. To what may they not confess her before they have writhed her into a bag of quivering pulp?"

"Enough, enough, enough, can nothing be done to save her? O, you whom all this persecution has left upright (and a refuge as men whisper to the threatened) from whatever source your commission comes, I wrap about me the hem of your mantle. Be your aid of God, or Devil, I invoke it!"

"Do you know what you ask? The Indians of Darian are charity, compared to me and mine. Be my aid of God, or Devil do you say? You shall rest in no doubt upon that head. The bare mention of the name of God is a source of danger among us of the opposition, save when we take it (for our own purposes) in vain. And of the opposition I have been, am, and shall be. That with which surmise is rife be here with certainty known to you! You treat with one having authority deputed from the Most High, the Prince of this World and of Hell."

"I have never shrunk from any, save one woman, and I do not shrink from you. In all this storm you are my sheet anchor."

"Then in my character of the Devil's proxy I offer you your heart's ease in tender for your soul!"

"In the event of my agreeing to your proposition how do you set to work to save her?"

"By the substitution for her of a *golem*, a device that I learnt from a *rabbi* of Provence that was my teacher in the art of *cabala*. It is a doll of wax (or indeed of any substance), no matter how uncouth, and upon the forehead of which in angelical letters one writes a chosen name—in your case the name Lisalda—I shall then conjure for you in a strong circle. You will clinch the bargain with my master in person by striking hands with him. And his claw will leave you for your lifetime branded with his private brand.

"This done he will breathe upon the *golem*. Obedient to the breath of life it starts (to all outward appearance) into a perfect double of the person in whose name it may have been inscribed.

In your case the name Lisalda. Nor will you yourself be able to tell whether Lisalda or the devil's coin stands before you. You will forgive my suggesting that in some respects you might be better off with the ideal than the real, since it starts in life (like a child) with a clear slate and you may teach it in what sort you will."

"How now! Do you libel my love?"

"I speak but as a man of the world and to some extent of the next world also. However, to resume our ways and means. My prince having bestowed upon the *golem* such life as it is only his and God's to give, I then smuggle the innocent know-nothing into the prison of your Lisalda and carry off Lisalda in exchange. Then to horse and hey for love and leisure— on the further side of the Bidassoa; but the cheat will never be discovered, and in fine and in finish the *golem* will run to ash like so many of her betters."

"Is there no other way?"

"There is no other way. Bethink yourself. The offer is there to take it or leave it. Shake hands with my master or shake your fist at him. Be one of us or one of her executioners."

"I cannot boggle long at that. Death of my soul! Have with you then Aquelarre and let fruition crowd the heels of haste."

"There is yet one thing that you may boggle at. You have ratified the bargain with my master but not the fee of my procuracy. You cannot do anything without me and I cannot do anything without that ring which you wear upon your finger as my handsel."

"Your fee is a fleabite to your master's. The ring I wear is yours but not as earnest money. I pass it over to you only after service rendered. And now lead on to this *golem* you speak of."

"Be it as you say. The preliminaries being all settled between the high contracting parties, I usher you to the actual presence of my principal."

As he thus concluded the negotiation a covetous light (like to nothing in heaven or earth) shot through the lashes of the devil's attorney. He stood at last upon the brink of attainment of that ring so thirstily craved. With an imperious gesture he summoned the sailor to follow him and turned off behind the staircase. Directly the sorcerer's back was turned Ataurresagasti could not forbear a broad grin. He had outwitted (at any rate he thought so) both the infernal furious spirit and his attorney. And first as to the latter. The fact was that the only ring worn by the sailor himself, and pledged to Aquelarre by the letter of the bond, was a tawdry hoop of silver. The ring that contained the familiar had never left the dead man's hand.

How then had the inn-keeper imagined otherwise? Simply because the sailor, with a view to better protection, had drawn up his right arm within his sleeve and held the Hand of Glory by the wrist in such a position as to appear his own. The ring which thus appeared to adorn the sailor's little finger was in reality still upon that of its architect. And, therefore, it was still un-pawned to Aquelarre. But this was not the only or even the first fruits of the trick which Ataurresagasti (or his good angel) had set in motion. As he gathered from the sorcerer that the devil would imprint his private mark upon him by means of a grip of hands, Ataurresagasti (or, again, his good angel) jumped at once to the obvious deduction that by going through with the same sleight of hand, Beelzebub would come claw to claw with only the dead Cabalist and earn no soul but his.

Earn no Soul but his, which was undoubtedly already long-earned and already in heats of hell. Thus, by a single piece of hugger-mugger, the buccaneer hoped to go free with his sweet-heart and do no harm to anyone. Or, at any rate, to anyone that stood within the reach of harm, the only sufferers being the devil and his lost. How the whirligig of time brought round its revenges the sequel of this story will show. Now that the reader is conversant with what was passing through the mind of the sailor we must return to where we left him at the back of the staircase.

Aquelarre, stooping down, by some device which the sailor did not fathom, raised one of the stone slabs of the flooring from its place. This impromptu trapdoor disclosed a flight of steps that fell down into absolute darkness. A motion from the land-lord and Ataurresagasti fearlessly stalked down them to some distance, where he stopped until he had seen his confederate also enter. Aquelarre drew down the trapdoor after him. This last action was fatal, of course, to such light as had previously washed the upper part of the stairs. All was now equal night. Yet the buccaneer continued his descent. The steps seemed endless. At last he stopped. He listened. To his surprise and horror no footfall sounded above. What had become of Aquelarre? The sailor suspected some deception put upon him. He retraced his steps as quickly as was possible under the difficult circumstances of the ascent. That he reached the top was made apparent to him by the crash of his head against the stone. He reeled and all but fell.

What had become of Aquelarre? Recovering himself he tried with all his might to obtain egress but not unnaturally without avail. He mopped his brow and tried to think. Escape being impossible in this direction he decided to recommence the descent; come what might he could be no worse off than where he was even if he went down, down, down to the earth's centre. He tried to persuade himself that worse things happen at sea, but his heart of hearts nailed the lie. Down, down, down! He counted (as he thought) a thousand steps but not without dizzy doubts. And then he lost all count—all doubt—all but damned certainty. He had never been sick at sea but now—and then suddenly he staggered against some obstacle. It yielded. It was a door. Firelight danced in his eyes. He rolled into a corner and stood up against a wall. He was in an underground chamber and before him was Aquelarre.

How the devil's advocate had got there before him who can tell? Doubtless in some devil's way. Aquelarre made no remark upon the sailor's entrance nor ceased from his work of drawing (on the ground) circle within circle, distant from one another about a hand's breadth. The sailor rubbed his eyes and looked about him. The space (at one end of the vault) reserved for the circles was scrupulously clean, as well it might be, since one speck of pollution would have nullified their every virtue. The rest of the subterrane was a hotchpotch of horrors—the *disjecta membra* of a magical laboratory scattered broadcast over every inch of the floor.

Here were receptacles of unsightly shapes, crucible and cucurbit, alembic and aludel. Here were the spoils of charnel-house and churchyard, ear and eye; excrement and entrail. Here squat phials bore charges of price, poison and philtre, *lac virginis*, and *elixir vitae*. In one corner gibbered a gigantic skeleton. In another lay a Jacob's Staff and a Pentacle of Solomon. In a third helped up musty vellums, presumably occult; and of these, last Ataurresagasti picked up one, and was about to open it at random, when Aquelarre turned suddenly white, and fetched a roar so sudden that the startled sailor dropped it as if it burnt him. The magician (who had just finished inscribing his series of circles) came forward with a brow of night. His fist was clenched as if to strike. But after glaring some moments at the buccaneer, he twisted his nails out of his palm again where they left four bleeding scars. He calmed down still farther before he could speak.

"Madman let this teach you never more to tamper with such wild-fire as a magic book. There are spells on every page of that volume which (had you exposed even one of them to the air) would have dissolved us both into death and hell. It is easy to see that this is your maiden bout as sidesman to an exorcist. Were you an ordinary neophyte, even your failure to play Paul Pry, would have quenched you the light of day. But take heart of grace and fear nothing mortal, for on your life great issues hang. But lest you should make another slip (and perchance to perdition) mark well what I am now about to teach you.

"And firstly, to install our *golem*—yonder it hangs in the fourth corner of the vault, suspended and swinging above our heads. You ask me why it so suspends and swings. I will tell you. Look at its forehead and you will see a name, which if you could read our angelical letters you would find to be the name of De Lancre, of the Parliament of Bordeaux. De Lancre, that is the torturer of our wizardry and of your bride, and the touchwood of a thousand fires that depopulate Labourt. But his turn shall yet be served. By the sympathy which I have established between this mannikin and him (by only the sealing of it with his name) I have got into my hands more power over his body than your untortured fancy would conceive.

"I could even bring his life to a close at this very second, by piercing his heart with a pin. But at the moment I am content by this swinging between earth and sky (as they say swings Mahomet's coffin) to afflict him with horrors, to which death were meat and drink,—to afflict him with dizziness, vertigo, and whirlpool, with falling sickness and ceaseless belching, yea, to the innermost membrane of his soul. But that your need of this lay figure is greater than his, he should sleep never a wink tonight. Nay, not all the drowsy drinks of the herbal should gum his eyelids up. But behold I release him and lean him against this wall, and erase his name with my finger. 'Tis done, and De Lancre at the very instant far away is restored to perfect health. Some charlatan will doubtless get the credit for a cure."

He broke into a peal of horrible laughter. But the sailor scarcely heeded. He was gazing at the figure which he understood was to be transformed with a blasphemous breath into an exact simulacrum of his betrothed. A greater difference than at present existed between the two could scarcely be imagined. Lisalda was—well we will not attempt the impossible task of reproducing a lover's raptures. The *golem* was a rude lump of modelling wax with five projections, occupying respectively such parts of the main body as suggested that they were meant for its legs, arms, and head. The last distinguished itself from the four limbs by several additional clues to its identity.

It had eyes indicated by a couple of stones. It had ears, or, at any rate, handles, on either side, and a third in front for nose. It had a mouth which left even more to the imagination, since its hieroglyphic was a herring bone. Lastly, it was thatched (somewhat scantily, it must be confessed), with what appeared to be the bristles of a hog. With a view no doubt to decency, the devil's attorney tied a rag about its middle. Another about its right arm he explained as representing the prison bandages which swathed the tortured limb of the real Lisalda. Finally, he inscribed upon its brow a name, and declared it to be complete. And now for a lesson in ceremonial magic.

Seven circles Aquelarre had compassed, waxing smaller and

smaller within each other. In the innermost (which is where the two daring exorcists should stand) the devil's advocate placed a pan of coals, the same that had hitherto only given light to the room, but of which the real use and purpose was suffumigation. This suffumigation was that part of the work which was to fall to the lot of Ataurresagasti. For this the landlord placed beside the pan various packets of perfumes each numbered in the order with which they were to feed the flames. And woe unto the exorcists, if in the flurry of even one second Ataurresagasti changed the order of succession. They had better have never been born! And now Aquelarre girt him with his magic sword and hung a pentacle about his neck. The time had come to pass the series of circles.

"Put off thy shoes from off thy feet, for the place whereon thou standest is holy ground."

Ataurresagasti assimilated himself to the guise of companion. He entered the inmost circle. Aquelarre took once more his crayon and inserted within each circle (one and all being yet in blank) a symbol illegible to the sailor, but which the devil's advocate translated as he proceeded somewhat as follows:

"The name of the hour wherein you do the work, the name of the angel of the hour, the seal of the angel of the hour, the name of the angel that rules the day in which you work and the names of his ministers, the name of the present time, the names of the spirits ruling in that part of time and their presidents, the name of the head of the sign ruling in that time."

This done all appeared to be in order and the exorcism forthwith commenced. Aquelarre commanded the sailor to cast the first packet upon the flames ("and unwrap it not lest it skin thy hand"); the which being done the former brightness of the light burns directly a hideous red of leaping blood and every object in the room tinges to match. The magician draws his sword and makes passes with it in his right hand. He places his left upon the pentacle on his breast and commences in the following strain:—

"In the name of the holy, blessed, and glorious Trinity proceed we to work in these mysteries to accomplish that which we desire. We, therefore, in the name aforesaid, consecrate this piece of ground for our defence, so that no spirit whatsoever shall be able to break these boundaries, neither be able to cause injury, nor detriment to either of us here assembled. But that he may be compelled to stand before this circle and answer truly on demand, so far as it pleaseth Him who liveth for ever and ever, and who says I am Alpha and Omega, the beginning and the end, which is and which was, and which is to come—the Almighty. I am the first and the last who am living and was dead, and, behold! I live for ever and ever, and I have the keys of death and hell. Bless, O Lord, this creature of earth wherein we stand. Confirm, O God, thy strength in us so that neither the adversary nor any evil thing may cause us to fail."

The chant of the magus grows shriller and shriller, till it thins into a final continuous shriek. And there mingles with it thunder, and the re-echoed echo of shriek and thunder, to the splitting of ear and brain. And the earth rocks until there remains no longer floor nor roof, but sometimes one was uppermost and sometimes the other, and only the rapidity of the motion makes it possible to keep place in the circle. Thus, alternately, the venturous pair stood erect or head downwards. In this part of the ordeal, however, the sailor's professional habit stands his friend in need; but his teeth were twisted out of rank by clenching, to avoid a cry. The fire (now yellow) burns foul in the nose and hangs upon the hair in folds of smoke. Ceaseless lightnings lash the streaming eye.

Clothed as it were, in those folds of smoke, there gradually appears to incorporate itself a large, full, and gross body—sanguine and gross—in a gold colour, with the tincture of blood its motion is like the lightnings of heaven; the sign of its becoming visible is that it moves the person to sweat that calls it; the sorcerer becomes mute before the majesty of that presence and the thunder is hushed in its breath. There creeps a claw from out the draping clouds and steals towards the right hand of the sailor—say the right hand of the Cabalist rather, for it is that which the sailor clasps fearlessly to the arch fiend's itching grip. A second's compress—a grit of bone against bone—a hiss, as of a branding iron, and the talon is withdrawn.

The sailor gazes appalled for a moment at the blackening, indelible sign manual, now seared upon the palm of the Cabalist. His heart of hearts sings a *paean* of victory over a lie palmed off upon even the Father of lies. The blowing of the Fiend now falls upon the *golem* and a gradual inflation swells out that pitiful suggestion into full and female form. Eyes like orbs of night light the vault and outburn the yellow jealousy of the brazier. Ears like seashells, and teeth like pearls of the sea, hair that paragons Godiva. O God, and is this but a counterfeit that can so kindle our sailor's senses? But he is recalled to gruff reality by the sight of her prison dress and bleeding bandaged arm.

He is about to step out of the circle when a buffet from his companion fells him like an ox to the ground, scattering splashes of yellow flame in his fall. The magician indicates by signs rather than words, that the devil called up has yet to be laid before either of the callers can venture forth with safety. And then Aquelarre proceeds with full strength of lung (lest haply further risk betide) to recite the accepted form of dismissal.

"Go in peace unto your place. Peace be between us and you. Be you ready to come when you are called."

Ataurresagasti awakened to his sense of duty, sacrifices yet another packet of incense. Blue of heaven burns the flame, and sweet the savour that (after a struggle) overpowers its predecessor. The prince of fallen pride dissolves into fulgurant reek. Earth recovers its footing. The fire at last resumes its work-a-day tone. Nothing but a grateful suspicion of the incense still about the convalescent air remains to betray what manner of work has been done. And now with assurance the exorcists may leave circle. Aquelarre cannot forbear to bring home to his sidesman the gravity of that false step he nearly made.

"Should your stars ever fate you again to dally with infernal fire, be never tempted to leave your circle until the spirit is dismissed; nay, even when the spirit refuses to appear at your call you must still formally dismiss him according to the rules of art, lest haply he be actually present (though to you invisible) with intent to pluck your soul."

"'Tis a lesson I shall never need to learn again."

"But now to the next step in our progress. From the opposite end of this vault to that by which you entered there is a subway to the condemned cell. Many a time and oft has this been useful to me before, for you need not plume yourself the first that has self-sacrificed upon the altar of his love. Parent or child—lover or spouse—have employed me as middleman over and over again. My memory teems triumphant with case after case where the burners, unknowingly have burnt but the shadow of a witch. And so, shall it be again. I take the *golem* with me and rejoin you with your prize."

He touched a spring in the opposite wall which threw open the indicated door. The bottom of a flight of steps appeared, the pendant of that which the sailor had descended. Aquelarre took the apparently bewildered *golem* by the hand and with her disappeared. The door closed with a vicious snap. The sailor was left alone in a chamber hermetically sealed and Heaven knows how far beneath the foundation of the tavern of the Four Cross Roads. There were none of mortal kind around save bones of unshriven suicides who dreamed of judgment and woke up shrieking that they made the blood of youth run cold to hear them. These were his brothers in exile. He was fain to shout aloud, that corner to re-echoing corner of the vault might make him colloquy.

But was this jangled terror his that they groaned into his ears? Was this the note to which the lung of storm gave precedence in happier days upon the sea? How long this weird conversation lasted the sailor never knew. At length his straining ear caught the footfall which he had dared so much to hear again. To snatch Lisalda into his arms as she entered, to feel that she yielded to his embrace was breath and blood to our hero. But the devil's attorney touched him on the shoulder. He pointed sternly to the other door that led again to the inn. In Indian file (there was room for but one on a step) all three commenced the ascent. How quickly it sped compared with that well remembered descent. But the sailor found time to hide in his waistband the Cabalist's branded hand.

When they reached their wonted level Aquelarre closed the

trap, and throwing open the door of the street disclosed (he did not do things by halves) a fully caparisoned horse waiting outside. His whole face brightened into a smile of supreme content with himself and (for the nonce) all the world. His work was done. He held out his hand for the payment. The sailor did not smile. He took the silver ring ostentatiously from his little finger and placed it upon that of the devil's attorney. The face of Aquelarre underwent a very sudden change.

"Gates and gulfs of Hell! Do you realise with whom it is you jest?"

"Jest do you say? It is sober, serious, earnest."

"What the devil's name! You pledged me the ring you wear on your finger."

"I pledged it to you and I have passed it you—the only ring I ever wore—but if you refer to the ring of the demon, that has never left the dead man's; hand since for its sake you left him dead."

Before Aquelarre could recover from his stupefaction at this thunderbolt, Ataurresagasti swept Lisalda into the crupper and sprang to the saddle in front of her. And then loose rein and bloody heel, they dashed down one of the cross roads from which the tavern derived its name. Ride, ride, ride. Dark though the way and cold the wind, Ataurresagasti rolls a name upon his tongue that lights the path and warms the ambient air. Lisalda! Lisalda! Lisalda! Shock snowy polls of Pyrenean hills start up behind the haze. The lights of Behobia star the drift. Its cobbles fly to sparks beneath the horse's hoofs. The river cuts athwart the highway; the bridge is reached. Another stride and the *fleur de lys* is left behind for good. A customs officer leaps out of his box and seizes the horse's head; he is dragged several yards along the track. A torrent of imprecations in Basque, French and Spanish.

Ataurresagasti pulls his mount back on to its haunches. The officer is ultimately convinced that he is no smuggler, and relinquishes somewhat charily his prey; Ataurresagasti winds gently along the bank. When, beyond the range of pry or spy he dismounted and swung Lisalda to the ground. Once in his arms he did not readily let her go but showered kiss after kiss. The horse unheeded proceeded to explore on his own account and soon was lost to sight. Ataurresagasti showered kiss after kiss upon her wounded arm, her neck, her mouth, her eyes, her brow; but what is this—his lips are blistered in contact with the hair that shades that brow; he pushes the hair aside.

A name in fiery angelical characters is flaring there. Horror of horrors, 'tis the *golem*! In his far off tavern Aquelarre is laughing in his sleeve. Ataurresagasti stands aghast. The creature regards him with puzzled; eyes. She does not understand this sudden change; her mouth smiles and the first word she has ever uttered crosses her lips. It is her own name picked up, parrot-like from the iteration of the sailor. It had a different effect from what the poor thing expected.

"Lisalda!"

His cry of agony jarred her dulcet note. Every cord of his body was strung in an instant to one thought. To destroy this soulless creature—to annihilate—to erase her—to have her from God's earth. He pounced upon her. But the poor pretty monster seemed to feel by instinct that this was another guess embrace from the first ardent one. And instinctively she wrestled with him. It was an awful unheard-of bout. Not a syllable was spoken, nor a cry. The blood now streamed like rain from her wounded arm. They slipped in the puddling soil. And Ataurresagasti could not get rid of the horrible idea that it was, after all, the real Lisalda that he was; wiping out of life.

Bit by bit, and one by one he obliterated the cursed characters. And bit by bit as the execution proceeded a horrible change came over her. Her limbs grew lean and spidery that she twisted about him. Her eyes grew dull and fishy. Her hair fell out by handfuls. She was dying letter meal. At length he forced her to his feet still clinging to his knees. The last figure of the angelical name disappeared beneath his thumb. Before him there lay no longer She but It. No longer a Lisalda, but a battered waxen doll with two pebbles and a herring-bone clapped on to one side of its head to distinguish front from back. Laughable—yes, perhaps—but Ataurresagasti did not laugh.

He fell upon his face and wept. Something like an hour

passed before he rose. Then drawing his hanger, and selecting the greenest spot, he proceeded to dig a grave. This he lined with masses of such wild flowers as he could find, and then reverently disposed the *golem* upon them. He shovelled back the earth upon the body, as he could not help but call it. He stamped it down obliterating all traces of his handiwork. He had said no prayer, but prayers crowded into his mind. He seemed in his tangled consciousness to have buried the real Lisalda, and with her all his love. He drew towards the river and stared into its inscrutable depths, turning over in his mind the pro and con as touching suicide.

But after mature deliberation he decided, in preference, to return to that officer at Behobia, and give himself up for wife murder. He took a gloomy pleasure in this idea, and might even have carried it through. But suddenly a mocking peal of laughter—fiendish laughter —struck, as he thought, familiarly on his ears. He rubbed his eyes and looked across the river. On the French side of the boundary stream, there stood facing him the devil's attorney, hand in hand with what the now crazed sailor took for a *golem*. The existence in the world of a real Lisalda never occurred to his wandering wits. Aquelarre knew full well what had transpired. The sight of the discomfiture of his rival seemed balsam to his wounded self-esteem. Nor did he evidently as yet despair of making all things square. He addressed Ataurresagasti at first with real or assumed jocularity.

"*Hola?* master gaff topsail, and have you found the truth of what I once told you, that two can play in a game of brag? Come, we are surely quits by this time. Let bygones be bygones, and let us adjust our contra accounts. You hold on your side what is of value to me, and I on my side what is of value to you. Exchange is no robbery. Cast me the ring across the stream, and Lisalda shall join you at Behobia."

"Lisalda, do you say? And do you really think to befool me with a *golem*, in the making of which I myself had a hand? Lisalda, I know, is dead. By this hand she died, and I would cut it from me were it not that the bloody crust on it is the only relic of her that remains to me."

"Madman, you rave! Oh this I never dreamed of, that his reason should wander so untimely. Pull yourself together, man. 'Tis no *golem* that stands beside me. 'Tis your own Lisalda,— your cutest medicine—could I but get you to take it. Oh, be but for an hour sane, and then put eternity out of joint if . you will! Again, I say, the ring across the stream, and take Lisalda in exchange; that turns the scale against your immortal soul!"

"Never waste your lies on me, man! 'Tis nothing but a *golem* that you seek to palm off upon me. Lisalda, I know too well, is dead—by the token that these same impious hands that snatched her into darkness have just smothered her into a heathen grave. I had thought to have bedded her in other guise, but it seems my fondest star had never appraised me as so worthy. Take away your *golem*, and I shall keep the devil's autograph."

"Perdition be your speed! This passes patience. All is indeed at an end between us. All save my vengeance. For I will tell you now a secret that shall open your eyes to the imminent deadly breach between us. This Lisalda (whose name you would add to the long list already tattooed upon your hairy bosom) has not, does not, nor will ever love any other but myself. Sacristan at my Sabbaths from her earliest years—my living altar at the Black Mass—she is more to me than all your ring. Nay the very plot and plan for conveying that ring from its rightful owner was conceived and carried out by her.

"For that she undertook a special trip to the New World; for that she donned the disguise in which she wormed herself into the confidence of the Cabalist, and ultimately persuaded him to visit me at the Four Cross Roads. Unfortunately (you gentle-man swab) you took it into your cursed costard to see further into a millstone than other people. We tried to make account of your sea-dogged persistency by drugging your nightcap with a view to palm you off upon justice (save the mark) as the mur-derer of the Cabalist. But again, through your ferreting foresight (darkened be your eyes), you tripped upon the tragedy in the worst possible moment (trust you for that), and even blundered into possession of the ring. And now keep your ill-gotten gear, and Aquelarre for the first time in life is content to lie bought and sold."

He broke off abruptly as if unable to contain himself, and throwing himself upon the girl with ferocious ardour he covered all her face with kisses. Kisses that absolutely foamed at the mouth. Kisses which she with even greater abandonment returned. Ataurresagasti caught fire at the sight (as mayhap it was intended with devilish cunning that he should) and cried out across the stream, every muscle of his face quivering with jealousy.

"This is the stroke that beggars fate! All is indeed at an end between us! Bought and sold! Ataurresagasti is bought and sold! But I can touch you in what (in spite of all you say) I know is still a raw. The devil bless you, and thus to the devil with demon and ring!"

"Stop, stop, stop! 'Tis no hand of the Cabalist upon which the ring sparkles but the hand of his murderess whom you love! Through you in your ignorance it was branded with the brand of Beelzebub, and if you relinquish it her soul will be struck from her!"

He crowded the words together incredibly in his eagerness, but yet he was too late. The Hand of Glory now acknowledged to be hand of Lisalda, had already left the sailor's touch. It flew through the air and as it flew, shot a double lightning of great joy. For the Demon (so long imprisoned within the crystal) knew at length that his appointed hour was come. Too late, the sailor grasped the stupendous revelation of Aquelarre. Too late, he recognised Lisalda in the supposed *golem*, and in Lisalda the murderess, whose shorn hand he had so long carried about him.

The moment that he hurled it violently from him a startling change took place in the girl. Her garments became shaggy hair. Her glorious eyes narrow and slanting. Her teeth protruded at great length and yellow. Name of Mercy! This was then that large and loathly wolf (a werewolf as he now astounded saw) that had scattered the life of the Cabalist. The huge incredible beast (with a mournful howl that curdled the sailor to the marrow) sprang desperately after the brand which bound her soul. But being short of one paw she failed to arrest it. The Hand of

Glory crashed down upon the water with an impact that shivered its crystal setting. It burst with a flame and smoke, and a hellish explosion with which mingled the dying shriek of the werewolf.

With a roar that made rock the whole Pyrenean chain, the demon thus set free had darted upon her! He shot up as it seemed through her very body in a column like a waterspout that seemed to pierce the skies. She was instantly riven into a million shreds and sprinkled in a red rain as far as eye could reach over the length and breadth of the stream.

The Rabbi Lion

The clock of the Jewish quarter of Prague moves in the opposite direction to its brethren of the Christian town, yet each in its own way arrives second by second at the same inexorable facts of time.

It was an hour short of midnight by both baptised and unbaptised reckoning—a misty rain was falling and mingled with the mist that rose from the river. Black obscure clouds veiled the face of the moon. Thunder roared at intervals. A flash of lightning that lifted momentarily the edge of the darkness revealed nothing kindlier than a gibbet. Dead bones that once had lived were creaking in its chains. The flesh had taken wing, the fowls of the air knew whither. Another flash showed a living man who crouched smothered up in a cloak at the foot of the unsightly tree. This unhappy outlaw if he dared seek no choicer shelter was, perhaps, even more to be pitied than his brother above. Whatever his reason, he made no motion in the direction of a light that shone afar and presaged warmth and shelter.

It was an inn. Its occupants concern us. They consisted of a company of half-a-dozen youths that had palpably imbibed both long and deep. Their carouse, however, was drawing to an end. The landlord hovered near cogitating over his bill, and yet with an ear to the conversation of his guests, lest haply he might catch some word. In this he was unsuccessful, and no wonder. The language they spoke was not only foreign to the landlord, but was that one of all others of which the angels themselves are traditionally supposed to be ignorant. In a word, it was Chaldee.

But how did these youngsters come to speak in the secret language of Cabala? The reason is not far to seek. They were students of the Cabala and of magic under a *rabbi*—one of the most esteemed of his time. The occasion they were celebrating with the flowing bowl was, indeed, no other than the conclusion of their seven years' apprenticeship. So far so good. But there was more in it than that. There was a death's head at their feast. Something that necessitated for its discussion their gift of tongues, something that took the heat from food and made the red wine show white through their skins. Upon entering their course, they had set their hands in blood to the customary indentures of the magical schools of that period.

After seven years (so the bond provided) only five of the pupils were to leave their Alma Mater their occult education complete; the sixth was forfeit to the devil, his due for acquiescence and assistance in their studies. A point on which the academies differed was the method of selecting among the apprentices which was to suffer as damned soul. Some held a kind of glorified race in which the runner that last attained the winning-post was torn asunder by the fiend. But the *rabbi* who conducted the reading party in which we are interested had laughed at a decision made on physical grounds.

The graduates should be chosen (he thought) not for fleetness of foot, but for the foremost quality of their sorcery. The scapegoat should similarly be thrown out not for unsoundness of wind or limb, but for the inadequate result of Black Art cramming. Logical enough all this. There remained but to discriminate between the competitors. To do this the *rabbi* had decided that on the morrow of the night when our story opens, he would hold a solemn incantation. It would be the first serious function of which the neophytes could boast.

Their seven years' candidacy had been occupied with theory and had never ventured on practice. They would now find out the difference between knowing how to raise the devil and doing it. A difference which is even greater in this particular case than between word and deed in other arts and sciences. The idea of the *rabbi* was that beginning gradually the terror should be accumulated ever thicker and faster until it reached a point where one of the men would break. This then would be the victim to be forced instantly from his circle and snatched soul from body by the enemy.

The reader is now cognisant of the mysterious business that fluttered these young hearts. We may add that their use of a dead language had another source besides the need for secrecy. No two of these ill-fated ones were natives of the same country, no two of them spoke a common speech. Such was the cosmopolitan fame of the *rabbi* at whose feet they sat that he could pick his lads from Arctica to Cancer.

We have already remarked that the supper drew to an end. The six had tried their manfullest to drown care, but they had found it impossible to get rightly drunk in the shadow of Death and of Hell, With despair for their toastmaster they drank every time the health of five, and thought the more that they spoke no word of the eternal ruin of the sixth. The roofless wretch outside was less to be pitied than these. They had discussed without hope every loophole of escape and hopeless rejected all. There was nothing for it now but to return home. The *rabbi* would never have allowed them out so late on any less momentous eve, but he had no fear of losing them now they had run out their course of lessons. He had done his part, they had received their consideration, trust him to look after his own that keeps the tally of the damned.

The reckoning had been adjusted to the satisfaction of the landlord, by the chairman of the feast. That youth (who was apparently a Bohemian by birth) now led his companions out of the house which someone of them was never to re-enter. And each turned back to look at it uncertain to what tune beggarly Fortune next might dance. They proceeded in the direction of the gallows we have already alluded to. Rain was still falling. The outlaw had disappeared, but will turn up later in our path. As they approached the grisly standard even the seasoned nerves of the sorcerers were troubled at the sight of its charge. They would have turned aside but for the Bohemian, who sturdily harangued them on their cowardice.

"The Devil walk arm in arm with you! Is this the way you stand to your guns at the sight of a gutted envelope—of a cast peascod—you that are due in but a few hours' space to outfront the root of all evil! I tell you the pit is digging deep for him that shows such favour then. But my liver is of another colour. What, fear a sloughed garment, and more rags than ribbons at that! Why I have only to set my hand to it"—

The incident ended in a manner entirely unforeseen. The Bohemian had barely touched the corpse when it dropped upon his shoulders. At this the other sorcerers shod with fear incontinently fled. The Bohemian stood his ground for only a moment. It had been in his mind that the thing would fall to pieces, but when he felt a burning breath, and the bony arms closing round his throat his brave soul shrunk like the kernel of a nut, and rattled against his sides. With the horrible revenant ever tightening its grasp the Bohemian started to flee. In doing this he followed in the footsteps of his companions, who had made their way back to the tavern.

The landlord was in the act of putting up his shutters when his late guests tumultuously helter-skeltered to his door, and shrieked for immediate rations of strong waters. Nothing loath he planted them again at his tables and exchanged their solids for his fluids. At this juncture the Bohemian appeared, alone, but sweating to the very palms. He steadied himself against the wall and drank off the landlord's proffer at a gulp.

"Your health!" cried out a mocking voice from the very midst of the convives.

The Bohemian dropped his glass with a crash that sowed its fragments wide. There was a stranger sitting in the midst of their company, and drinking as if one of themselves; no one had seen him enter. The host appeared as much at a loss as they were. But the unknown being obviously man of mortal mould the Bohemian soon recovered his wits. He challenged the unbidden guest.

"Who are you? And why do you drink to me?" The stranger rose to his full height, which was more than common tall. We repeat that none of those present knew him; but to continue our practice of dealing fairly with the reader we identify him with the outlaw with whom we commenced our story huddled up at the feet of justice. This understood, we record the stranger's speech:—

"Walls have ears, and if you would know me you must breathe the outer air. As to my drinking of your health, between man and man, do you not look as if you needed it?"

The obvious truth of this remark was only fuel to the Bohemian's fire. The more anxious on that account to know who the mysterious one was, he signed to his companions to come outside. The rain had now ceased. As they retraced—not without trepidation—the path they had so hastily left, they noticed that the gibbet was again occupied, but no one dared to ask the Bohemian how he had got rid of his unwelcome visitant It was the stranger who renewed the conversation by abruptly mentioning his name "I am Iron Haquin!"

His hearers started. They had expected nothing like this. It was a name proscribed, and upon which a heavy price was set. It was the name of the comrade (still at large)—of him that shook a leg on the gallows. But Iron Haquin knew that these men were nothing to be feared. The affair of the dead bandit had given them their fill—of thief-taking, at any rate— for that one night. The living might safely laugh them out of countenance about that exploit. He addressed himself accordingly to the Bohemian.

"What! frightened with the rattling of bones that ride the gale? Would have me believe that the unrepentant thief descended from the cross? A sorrow on your fears! Take such tales to your confessor, for I'll have none of them, be sure! You had looked too long upon the jewelled wine, and that's the long and the short of it. I'll even touch hands with my dead mate myself, just to show you how unfounded your stampede. You will see no windfall vouchsafed to me, shake I never so shrewdly the tree."

He suited the action to the word and the event proved him right. The sorcerers would have turned tail at half a suspicion. But never a miracle occurred this time. The corpse continued to hug its chains. The Bohemian waxed wilder and still more wild, but he did not cease to listen to Iron Haquin.

"Fear has no share in life of mine—death has been all too long my fellow—familiarity breeds contempt. I believe I could make the Devil's pulse jump could I only obtain an interview. That, at any rate, is the one thing left that might fathom the resources of my heart I saved the life of a Hebrew once, who, in return, gave me lessons in magic. I never worked so hard in my life. I looked to shortly kiss the mouth of Hell, but, as ill luck would have it, I quarrelled with my *rabbi*, and never found a chance."

The Bohemian could scarcely help showing his incredulity, nor did he care much for the stranger's feelings.

"What possible cause of quarrel could you have with a man whose life you saved?"

"Cause enough for anything and everything since he introduced me to his betrothed and I fell in love with her. He poisoned her mind against me, and on a chance cast me into a well. The water, however, was sufficient to break my fall, and I escaped after starving many days. It was twenty years ago, but I have never been able to forget it. He shall yet curse the mother that bore him. I tell you all this frankly as I told you my name, because I know that you are not what you seem!"

The Bohemian followed this relation, and chewed the cud of it. An idea had occurred to him fraught with unholy joy. He saw (as he thought) how he could achieve his own salvation at one stroke with the death of the intruder. How it worked out we shall see in the sequel. This is how the Bohemian set it going.

"What do you mean by saying that we are not what we seem?"

"Because, although your outer man is clad in this world's uniform, your hearts are of the livery colours: of Hell; you are students of sorcery, and no later than tomorrow you are to conjure in your strength. Do I not read you rightly?"

The Bohemian stared in something very much like stupor. Where on earth could the man have got his information? It sealed his death warrant, in any event He knew too much for sure! The Bohemian, by this time, had matured his plans, which he now expressed in words.

"Whatever your source of knowledge you have hit us off correctly, I admit; nor can we deny hospitality to such a man. We are within (as you say) a few hours of a magical ceremony. If you are so anxious as you pretend to face such odds I will go so far as to yield my place to you."

For the life of him the Bohemian could not help something of a smile as he made this handsome offer. He was ignorant still whether the bandit was aware of the exceptional nature of this incantation. His reply would decide that point. If he knew the rules of the approaching contest he would certainly refuse. If he did not, he could hardly maintain his fame without becoming a substitute for the Bohemian. To do him justice, Iron Haquin did not hesitate for a moment.

"Your hand upon the bargain, man, and never fear but I shall do you credit. Since the beginning of recorded time there shall have been no such conjuration. We will quench the light of adverse stars. Hell's idiom has no word for what we shall do."

Still wearing the same sardonic grin, the Bohemian broke in upon this enthusiasm. His department was the practical.

"Permit me to draw your attention to the fact that we have been drifting slowly on and shall soon have reached the *rabbi's* house. It befits us, therefore, to arrange our order of business. It may not have occurred to you that the *rabbi* must know nothing about this. If he did, he might possibly veto the affair. But there will be no difficulty in circumventing him. The house is built square around a central court where the conjuration will take place in open air. You will enter with us muffled in your cloak, and your presence will not be detected among so many; you will conceal yourself under the staircase while the *rabbi* takes us to our bedrooms, which are the topmost of the house.

"The old gentleman locks us in all night, for we are strictly looked after, I can assure you. When we are released (after a brief slumber) it will still be dark, and if I slip into your hiding-place and you assume my authority I do not see why the *rabbi* should be the wiser. As to the risk you run that is, of course, more your affair than mine. I shall pray for you from my coign of vantage if I can remember any but backward prayers. But now, confess, are you not moved at length with fear?"

"Nay, by horn and hoof! I shall weather the devil as I have got the weather of death, and be hail-fellow-well-met with both! At the worst a man can die but once— I had rather thus than a prod and a sod like so many that I have sent to their account. And, to end all, is this your destination? Why, it is the house of Rabbi Lion!"

"The Rabbi Lion is our teacher."

The Bohemian was only too glad that the matter was thus settled. His fears for himself, and of the other, were disposed of in one ingenious *coup*. The remaining five sorcerers had followed the negotiations with mixed admiration and envy. From them no remonstrance was to be expected, quite the contrary, since they believed and hoped that the bandit as a novice in magical matters would be the one to pay penalty to the fiend. They had yet to find out that their dupe had more knowledge than they bargained for. Meanwhile the Bohemian has knocked at the door. From within there comes a clangour of bolt and bars. The door is opened, and the *rabbi* appears. His pupils enter in as much of a hustle as possible, allowing Iron Haquin to conceal himself as arranged. The students file upstairs to be disposed of by their tutor, who will presently return alone.

During this absence of the *rabbi*, Iron Haquin took by the forelock the opportunity of looking around. The courtyard itself was bare, the lofty walls of the house built it in on all four sides. Under the roof half-a-dozen windows seemed to indicate the garrets of as many students. On the level of the ground there was nothing but two doors to break the monotonous courses of stone. One of these massive portals was that of the street through which Iron Haquin had entered. The other, which faced it on the opposite side, had been left ajar by the *rabbi*. It was of a certainty the passage way to his sanctum. The bandit approached it and looked through. A mighty chamber lay behind.

The light which streamed from it into the courtyard was engendered by a central lamp, one of that sort which are traditionally reputed to burn with an everlasting flame; from the ceiling hung stuffed reptiles and other grotesques that seemed to shiver in the current of fresh air. Tables conveniently disposed for work were loaded with books and manuscripts; every available niche and nook was piled with tools of necromancy that the bandit had no time to identify. Hearing the steps of the *rabbi* descending, he slipped to his covert just in time. The ancient Israelite re-entered his studio and slammed the door behind him. The wondrous light was thus extinguished, and the courtyard plunged in darkness. But not for long. The outlaw had scarcely disposed himself for sleep—better quarters this than the gibbet's foot—when the door was again thrown wide.

He looked in the expectation of seeing once more the *rabbi's* work-room; but to his utter surprise and consternation it was a different room altogether, though indisputably the self-same door. This time it was a lady's *boudoir* that was revealed, of immense size, imperially furnished—a thousand mirrors flashing back its chandeliers. There was no trace of the *rabbi* who had just entered that very door, instead, a beautiful girl of about twenty summers glided out to the cooling breeze. Had it not been for her Iron Haquin would have been dumbfounded at the inexplicable shift of rooms. But the moment he set eyes on her so much greater a surprise beset him that it drove all other out of mind.

It was the woman of whom he had spoken to the Bohemian—the woman who had cut friendship, and all but wrought his death—the woman whom still he loved. He strode forth without a second thought.

"It is her very self!" he cried.

The girl smiled at him as in recognition. Not the least surprise did she show at this strange meeting. She called him by his name.

"Iron Haquin!"

"You know me after all these years?"

"Who better among men should I know after all that passed between us? And did you not first know me?"

"That is not the same thing. I am twenty years older, but you—I can hardly believe my eyes—are the girl of twenty years ago. Has time, too, been fooled by those eyes of yours which I have often said would split a lover's coffin?"

"Believe me, my friend, Time's ravages are here as surely as that you will never see them. It is your love now, as ever, that blinds your eyes and drapes a faded woman in your poetry. When I am dead, and my body an ordinary for worms, you will see me still in fancy's eye just the girl you see me now. And by the same token you, that speak of being twenty years older, are in my eyes the brave and innocent boy whose lips were once my food."

"Then you loved me all the time, after all?"

"At that age, what did I know of love—or loathing?"

"But the *rabbi*?"

"He is old," she cried, "past passion. Ah, Haquin, you would not know him now!"

"I cannot make it out that you are still sweet and twenty. Here is a waist would warm the arm of death! You are, if any-thing, lovelier, transfigured, haloed. You would hurry the pace of a star! Tell me true now, is it not some elixir of the *rabbi's* that has pinnacled you beyond the teeth of Time?"

She laughed.

"Elixir of his! Why he would swallow it himself! And to prove how little I lean on him you may kill him if you will!"

"An assassination!" gasped the bandit, "the man knows no sword play."

He was thinking, as he spoke, of the primitive device by which his rival had once tried to get rid of him.

"A duel!" returned the Jewess, "for if he knows, no sword play he can measure swords with steel they forge below. You are a tall man of your hands when knives are stripping, but at his trade you are the *rabbi's* fool. You will need all you know to join issue with him in ceremonial of magic. No later than this morn-ing must you pit your strength against him, for to that you were decoyed hither."

"Decoyed! I came of my own free will, for an adventure to my mind. The story is worth telling. I was dying for a sensation, so I decided to cut down a comrade and give him more decent sepulchre than a gizzard. I had just got his corpse in safety to the ground when I heard a confusion of coming footsteps. Fearing it might be noticed that the gibbet was naked I swung myself into the chains. I knew from their conversation they were magical students that passed. I had a yearning to foregather with such once more, as I did in the days of my youth. A practical joke gave me the opportunity, and Heaven be praised for the good hap!"

Iron Haquin was about to improve the occasion, but, at this interesting juncture, a howl of rage discharged through the upper air. It came from the head of the Bohemian thrust out of his window. The Jewess snatched up the two hands of her lover and pressed them to her fervid lips. Almost before he was aware of it, she had retreated to her bower, and closed the door behind her. At the same moment the Bohemian, having wriggled through his window, leaped headlong into the courtyard.: He came down unskilfully. Iron Haquin thought he heard his leg go; He lay there groaning, and then burst into invective against the outlaw.

"The devil rough-ride you that have seen, so close, a dream I only sighted from afar. Bestride me the succubus, if I would have brought you hither had I known she would come out tonight. The skies are dark as a wolfs throat, and I believed she only walked in the moon. Full many a night I watched it shine on her silken hair—silken as the touch of sin—long, so that when she unbound it, she stumbled in her locks. Her silver body was fragrant as the boundaries of Hell. Death and dissolvement! Let me get you in my grips, and you shall never see her twice! Help me to my feet and unfold your blade, and then bite on what prayers you know!"

The bandit surveyed this unexpected rival with something very much like fellow-feeling. Then he voiced the question that was uppermost in him.

"How old did you suppose her?"

"How old? What do I care how old? Old enough to be loved and to love."

"How old did you suppose her?"

"If you insist on it, I suppose she wears some twenty years, and a queenly garment they!"

"What! Twenty years in your sight also! Why I tell you this very girl is the one of whom I spoke to you that I loved twenty years ago."

"You lie, by the Father of Lies!"

The bandit clapped his hand to hilt, and as instantly snatched it away.

"I fight with no cripple," he hissed in his teeth, "but you shall hear from herself God's truth!"

So saying he ran his great strength against that door. Twice and thrice he rammed it. It did not flinch. He went back a few steps to acquire a fresh impetus. But before he could return to the attack it flew abruptly open, as if moved by some hidden spring. Iron Haquin uttered an astonished cry. The *boudoir* was no longer there!

The mysterious chamber had undergone another Protean change. To speak more by the book, there was no longer any chamber. The door framed nothing but blackest darkness. Neither ceiling, nor walls, nor floor could be distinguished. By this time the Bohemian had struggled to his feet, and now hobbled in the direction of the door.

"Back, back," cried the bandit, "this is no place for you, nor for any christened man. The foundations of this house are laid in hell. Back, back, as you value your infinite soul!"

"To heel," shrieked the Bohemian, and he whipped out his sword, "lest I strike you in the place where you live! This is my hour, and you shall not be the only one to take her between your hands."

Before Haquin could forestall him, he had leaped the grinning door, and disappeared in enigmatical gloom. He was scarcely lost to sight, when a shriek rang out, beyond conception awful. It was his death-note. The whole air curdled. Iron Haquin fell upon his knees. What grimmest of riddles the victim solved no man shall ever know. His body—even as his soul—was lost in that abysmal horror. For a while Haquin gazed at it, and saw no sign, nor heard what could be called a sound. It was a grave that gave up no dead.

At last, the outlaw rose and crossed himself, and closed the door upon its secret. Withdrawn to his corner, he set himself to think what monstrous enigma couched behind there. The worst of it was that it threw still more suspicion on the woman. But was she a woman at all? In his wanderings across Europe, from sea to sea, he had never lost the Jewess out of mind. Whenever it was possible to acquire later news of her, he spared no pains to do so. But the gossip, through which alone at such a distance he could keep himself in touch with her circumstances, was always vague, and often contradictory. He had been circumstantially assured of her death, and as circumstantially undeceived.

But now he began to wonder if that report might have had foundation. To assume that upon losing her the *rabbi* had supplied her place with a familiar culled from the females of the pit, would explain nearly all that he had seen. Was it woman or nightmare that couched behind there? He had arrived at no decision when the door again flew open, and he stretched out his head for the next development. But the panoramic capacity of the door seemed, for the time being, to have played itself out. The view was only the old one of the laboratory out of which the *rabbi* stepped.

He was loaded with apparatus of ceremonial magic; he deposited it upon the ground; he closed the wonder-working door. His next step was to trace out two enormous circles, one within the other. The outer one embraced the whole area of the courtyard, the other one ran inside it at a distance of about a yard all round. Between the circumferences of these two circles he inscribed seven smaller ones, at equal distances apart. The outlaw, who, though disappointed at the drying-up of the resources of the door, watched all these proceedings with attention, perceived that the seven circles were intended—one each—for the *rabbi* and his six attendants. He concluded that the ill-starred Bohemian, as having been undoubtedly cock of the school, would be assigned one of the two circles next the master, which was precisely the post Iron Haquin would have chosen.

He was in some doubt, however, as to whether there might, or might not, be a miscarriage when the bedroom was found to be unaccountably empty. Fortunately, the *rabbi* (after placing a pan of living coal in each circle) went upstairs to unlock each door, and came down again at once, without opening any. This may have been intended to allow time for his disciples to dress, but he bore as well the air of one having forgotten something, and ran as fast as his years would permit him to that door of doors. The outlaw noted as the *rabbi* passed through that it was the *boudoir* this time visible.

Apparently, the thing worked round in a cycle. The *rabbi* emerged again almost at once with a look of considerable relief. All this was Greek to the onlooker. The five candidates now appeared and took up the circles pointed out to them. The outlaw pulled his hat well over his features, and (as it was still dark) hoped to pass muster. He saw, as he had expected, one of the places of honour was left for the Bohemian. He boldly took his stand there; he had now burnt his boats, and must go through. The *rabbi* had not yet syllabled a word, reserving his strength for the strain to come. He silently divided among his assistants the remainder of what he had brought out of his store room. This consisted of civet, amber and musk, of benzoin, camphor and myrrh, of every fragrance that wizards burn.

The *rabbi* then stepped into his own circle and commenced a preliminary prayer. The supreme moment had come.

A sudden glow invaded the veins of the amateur-exorcist (late Iron Haquin) as he heard that well-known voice. Bit by bit, as he warmed to the work, he remembered the ritual which this very man had once been at pains to teach him. From time to time the other five chimed in with the responses. Iron Haquin dared not risk the recognition of his voice. As the ceremony proceeded the air seemed to grow more dense until it became a matter of difficulty to breathe. It was thickening with, as yet, invisible elementals. *Anon* the outlaw's attention was drawn to the glances of his fellows, which timorously sought the empty space enclosed by the inmost of the two circles. He was somewhat dashed—even he—to see that this empty space had sunk below the level of the courtyard.

Worse, it continued to sink until it disappeared altogether. The magicians now stood in their seven circles, around the circumference of a well. Even this was not the worst, as the bottom, though out of sight, must still be sinking, and would sink to the very confines of the underworld. Connexion was to be opened with the bottomless pit by means of this bottomless shaft. Having arrived at this by no means engaging conclusion, Iron Haquin had only to wait for the end. It came with a sudden smother and smoke that belched from the mouth of the chimney. The *rabbi* threw instantly perfumes upon his fire, and his acolytes did likewise. Essence and quintessence fought desperately with the evil odours of this smoke that came straight from eternal fires.

And there was borne up with the smoke a weird hubbub of voices, that blasphemed in every tongue. Cracked lips of the damned shrieked execrations in languages long dead, whose accents unintelligible made heart stand still. In vain the *rabbi* raised his voice that had never ceased from the first onset. His exorcisms were drowned in oaths both loud and deep, and with the rush and roar of furnaces stoked with blood. And now the thick air showed faces that peered in their eyes, and gibberings that were not faces, creeping and crawling things. The outlaw's skin had long ago wrung out its last drop of sweat. The *rabbi's* white hair stood all on end. The moment for the trial had come.

Iron Haquin threw his hat out of the circle where it was instantly torn into a million shreds; His face thrust abruptly into the *rabbi's* line of sight, he roared in tones of thunder

"Rabbi Lion, I am Iron Haquin!"

The effect upon the *rabbi* was electric. His eyes started out of his head. The chant died away upon his lips. He dropped like a stone into the pit. One long low moan reverberated from side to side, broken up by peals of hellish jubilee. A terrible voice that hushed all else cried out three times—

"Lost! Lost! Lost!"

This was the climax, and Iron Haquin the man to bear the brunt of it. No help was to be expected from the five sucking sorcerers. They were ridden to rags. The last events had crowded so quickly together that the outlaw practically took up the litany where the *rabbi* dropped it He gave it such voice as would have been a surprise to the others, were they in a state to make the observation. The fact is Iron Haquin was drunk with the cup of revenge. For two pins he would have bearded the fiend. The infernals shrunk from the lash and lather of such magnificent rage expressed in the highest terms of art. They of the pit sucked in their smoke and hushed the outlet of despair. The centre of the courtyard reappeared, air refined itself, victorious sweet scents flung wide their banners.

"Go in peace unto your place. Peace be between us and you. Be you ready to come when you are called."

This final, formal leave-taking of the spirits, without which no magician worth his salt would ever abandon his circle, wound up what had once looked a serious business. The six could now quit in safety the circles which a moment before had been their only bulwark against perdition. The students were too limp to pay any attention to the giant that had taken their world upon his shoulders. Their little remaining sanity was all bent to the desire to get away from an accursed house. They stumbled out of the front gate, which the outlaw had to open for them, and scattered to the four winds of heaven.

The coast being now clear the bandit made for that other door which had played so many parts. On what would the curtain now arise? He opened and discovered the *boudoir*. A repetition of its last role. The cycle theory was thus effectually disposed of. There was nothing for it but that the door obeyed some arbitrary will. Scarcely its own. The *rabbi* was dead, and worse. There remained then only the Jewess. But where was she? The chamber had no, outlet. She could in no wise have left it. Our hero ransacked every corner, he upset, and set up, and upset again every priceless piece of furniture, tore down silk and satin, and threw jewels underfoot, ground beneath his heel the command of armies, and the price of the honour of queens. At last his eye was arrested by a common glass bottle, he was fascinated by it, he held it to the light, he all but dropped it. It contained the object of his search.

Yes, there was no doubt now of the death of his former love. No doubt but that the *rabbi's* diabolical art and craft had replaced her by a familiar spirit. This was the receptacle in which he confined the familiar at seasons when he was not in need of her. This was the familiar herself within the bottle, reduced most delicately small. She still wore the guise of his long-lost wife with which her master had endowed her. She still caused a pang to the iron heart of Haquin to see her down to such poor prison.

And she knew her power over him. She knew that he would find a way. She smiled at him divinely, she clasped her tiny hands in prayer to him. But he was aware that he must needs release her. He neither thought nor would have cared that, now her master was dead, once released there was no controlling her. It just had to be done. But how to set about it? The stopper was sealed down and with a talismanic character on the seal. It was the uttermost secret of the *rabbi*. Iron Haquin could not read it, and without reading it could never open the bottle. There remained but one avenue of escape—the bottle must be broken. With all the strength of his iron arm he dashed it to the ground. There was a tremendous explosion, a roar like thunder, a flash before his eyes.

Not a mirror in the chamber but was shattered and scattered. A rapidly enlarging female form escaped from the shards of the broken bottle. It lost as it enlarged all resemblance to the well-remembered Jewess. It became indefinite, it thinned into little more than a mist. It gradually disappeared, yet, as the last waft of it brushed his face the passionate lover thought he felt once more his sweetheart's lips. But he looked around and saw himself alone with solitude, and wreckage, and desire of death.

The Evil Eye

Our story opens upon a gloomy function; the burning of a gang of wizards and witches.

The bells were ringing, but it was a muffled peal, and the hammers were subdued that wrought the scaffolding in the market place. The steps of the citizens were as those that seek pleasure or plunder by night, and the very soldier trailed a pike most unsoldierly silent. A stranger, who, from the singularity of his appearance, would have attracted notice on any other occasion, today threaded unchallenged this German town.

Tall he was, worn down to the bone, gaunt and prematurely grey, hollow-cheeked and hollow-eyed. His dress might be described, with no great stretch of language, as little but nakedness visible. But it was sweet with the scent of the sea, and the roll of the sea was in his long legs, as he wound his way to the central square. He looked neither to the right nor to the left. Arrived at his destination he took no heed of the ominous carpenters, nor of the woodwork to which they were putting the finishing touch. He walked straight—and as if by instinct rather than by eye—into a certain tavern of those that debouched upon that place. He might have been supposed to be dumb as well as blind, since he merely made a pantomime expressive of hunger as he sank into one of the seats.

The landlord looked with doubt at his visible assets. A sad thing of the nature of a smile flickered upon the burnt and blistered visage of the sailor. He evolved a ¡coin from some miraculous hiding-place in the cobweb that was his apology for raiment. The landlord bit it, rang it, and bit it again. Ultimately, he appeared satisfied, and placed food before his customer. The speed with which it vanished would have justified an observer in antedating considerably the stranger's previous meal. Leaving a clean plate, he threw himself back in his chair and steadily regarded the landlord.

Then he asked, not without emotion,

"Don't you know me, old comrade?"

The landlord started as if shot "By all the saints and saintesses! *Marquard!*"

"Aye, Marquard it is; but not the Marquard you knew of old. It was an evil hour I ran away to sea."

"But why have you not returned these years?"

"Returned! He asks me why I did not return! I that—before I had been long enough aboard to be on good terms with my inner man—was captured by the Algerine! I that have been chained to an oar in the galley of Barbarossa every day of these years of which you speak! But pay no heed to what I say. There is news for which I burn. You have lived humdrum can tell me of her, for whose *coquetries* I lost patience and exiled myself."

"She lives," murmured the landlord, in a half-hearted way, and he looked upon the floor.

"She lives! And what of my rival that I thought she preferred to me?"

"*He* lives, if you mean the Hungarian, whose name we could never pronounce, and whom we used to call Teremtette from his favourite oath."

"Come, tell more about them both."

The landlord cast a troubled eye upon him, and again looked down. He spoke with distinct embarrassment.

"Prepare yourself for the worst, my friend. Remember that he of whom we speak was always a hobnobber with sorcerers, and a sorcerer suspect. After your departure he became a sorcerer confessed."

"And *she*, man! What of her?"

"Alas! She followed wherever he led, though the devil's shadow was all his light. She lived with him for a time after you abandoned the field to him."

"I knew it! In my dreams they were husband and wife, the while I hugged a bare board to my aching heart."

"Husband and wife! They were never that, save at some witches' sabbath, mated by priests unfrocked and anathematised, but not in the sight of gods or men."

"Then she is free, and I shall steal her from him yet. I will marry her, but I will kill him first."

"You know not what you say. He is swollen in power until he is acknowledged the master magician of all Germany. It is *whispered* that he made a pact with Satan, and in pledge thereof exchanged one of his eyes for an eye of the fiend's. It is *known* that he walks abroad with one eye shut until he wishes to perform some evil. Then he lifts the eyelid and shoots forth a spear of light from that eye which is not his own. And it blasts wherever it falls. For this reason, we call him the Evil Eye."

"His backbone shall be limp for me, his front abased, his star is set, his grave is dug, his flesh already rots! I will bury him in a church that he may hug false hopes of salvation, and then I will set my feet on his gravestone when I stand with *her* before the priest. He shall shriek curses from his coffin while I knit her life to mine, until the scandalised sacred earth shall spit him forth to those that lie in wait."

"Unhappy man, you are still dreaming of the girl you left behind! Do you not realise that, now years have rolled over her, she is a mother witch? Nay, there is worse that I had hoped to spare you. Did you not notice the stakes erected outside in the market place? Today a host of women, and not a few evil men, are to wipe out their crimes with the last payment. At this very moment the sad procession is entering the square. Do you recognise no prisoner among them?"

He threw open the door. It was even as he said. The sailor sprang to his feet and scanned the accused.

"I do not see him there!"

"Not *he*, he flies too high for judge or jury, the devil's true knight, hell sublimate! But look again. Do you not recognise one of the women?"

With a terrible foreboding Marquard strained his eyes, but saw no face that corresponded to his memories. They were, without exception, abominable hags that were to suffer. But one of them had at once recognised him. Recognised *him*, in spite of the awful change wrought by his captivity. The foulest *beldame* of them all stretched her skinny arms to him; Her cracked voice called his name.

"Marquard!"

An icy hand gripped the galley-slave's heartstrings. In that second he lived all the years since last, he had seen her. He saw (in his mind's eye) golden hair shade to grey, skin become parchment, roses and lilies scatter in dust. He recognised her, and he leaped forward to her like an arrow from a bow. The spectators parted in amaze, to right and left. Guards and executioners fell back from his foot and hand. He caught the outstretched hands of the witch in his. He devoured her with his looks, and she him. He was as one in a dream. He scarcely felt her press something round into one of his palms. She whispered so that he alone heard her:—

"Marquard! It is a charm I am giving you that has cost me dear. It will protect you from all evil, and especially from *him*. As you love me, never part with it while you live. I dare not wish you well lest my prayer should blast you. Goodbye, and think sometimes kindly of me."

He would have retained her, but she drew her fingers away, leaving with him that globular something to which he paid no attention. She kissed him with her eyes. He tried to speak, but words were choked in sobs. And now the soldiers, both horse and foot, bore down upon him. A cry of rescue was raised by some of the crowd that were interested in the prisoners. Others shouted them down, and shook their fists in Marquard's face. The wildest confusion reigned.

His rags were torn from his back. A hundred blades were thrust into his flesh. Those that had taken his part pulled him one way, the more law-abiding citizens pulled him another. His head swam, he lost his footing, he fell, and was trampled alike by friend and foe, in the pitched battle that was fought over his body. He lost consciousness, and knew no more.

When he recovered his painful identity, it was some time before he could remember what had passed. He was sick, as he fancied, from the rollings of the galley, and sore from the laying-on of the taskmaster's whip. It was the possession of a certain ball, which he still clutched in his palm, which, after he had stared at it for a while, led him back to truth. When, by degrees, he had recovered his memory, he tried to make out of what substance it was formed, but without arriving at any conclusion, he carefully stowed it away.

He was most puzzled by the fact that he was in a room. It was dark, so that a considerable time must have elapsed. He rose, and felt all round the walls. There was no doubt about it. Presently he came upon the door. He tried it. It opened. He was evidently not a prisoner. He stepped into a passage, and up to another door. This one was locked, but the key was in it. He turned it, and opening the door disclosed the square. The mystery was now solved. He was in the precincts of the tavern. He had been saved, perhaps from death, by his good friend, the inn-keeper.

The night was magnificently clear. A single star hung low in the ear of the moon. He looked all around the deserted place that during his swoon must have been the scene of butcherly justice. The remnants of the stakes were evidence that the decrees of the law had really been executed. A few fragments of charred bone were now all that remained of the girl he had loved, he seemed to scent the odour of burnt flesh in the air. Suddenly, he became aware that he was not alone in his contemplation of this field of blood. Some man was ferreting about the bases of the stakes, and sifting the human dust that paved the square. It needed no second look to tell the galley-slave who this was, so much keener than love is hate. It was the man—or more than man—of whom Marquard had conferred with the inn-keeper. It was the Hungarian—Teremtette—the Evil Eye.

For what then was he a-search among this life that had ceased to live? Marquard thought that he could answer this question. The ball of so much mystery had been given to him by the witch, as a charm that would protect from this very man. The association of the Hungarian with her made it probable that he was acquainted with her possession of it, and with its powers. Such being the case, it was a property that he must itch to lay his fingers upon. Perhaps he had even attempted, and failed, to obtain it from her while she was alive. At any rate it was this, presumably, which he was agog for on the scene of her death. As a charm it would be unconsumable by fire, and had Marquard not been before him the Hungarian might have attained his end. The one weak point in the theory was that it supposed the wizard ignorant of Marquard's return.

Yet this was not impossible, since surely even wizards have their limitations. Having decided upon this explanation of his rival's presence, Marquard burned to confront him face to face. He strode boldly out of his protecting doorway. The Hungarian heard his step, looked up, and sprang to his feet. The galley-slave noted with a thrill that one of his eyes was closed. It was the Evil Eye against which he was soon to test his powers of endurance. For the wizard had evidently recognised him at once. His whole face was writhen with diabolical glee. Slowly he raised the lid that covered the Evil Eye. There was a gush of blinding light from under that veil. The square was lit up as by noonday sun. The ray struck remorselessly upon the sailor. He stood erect unshaken.

Astonishment was legible upon the magician's features at this evident failure of his trusted weapon. He raised the lid to its fullest extent, and put all he was worth into the uncanny stare. But the sailor stood erect, unscathed. The charm was doing the work which its donor had foreseen, and doing that work right well. The galley-slave registered a vow never to part with it. Suddenly the magician dropped his eyelid, and the market-place once more was dark. He had apparently arrived at some decision, for now—for the first time—he spoke.

"Antlers of Belial! Do I see before me my old friend Marquard?"

"Your enemy to the hilts you see."

"You must pardon my defective sight which obliged me to call in the aid of science before I recognised you. Who would have thought of seeing you here? But now I know you I shall not readily part with you. You shall sleep under no other roof than mine this night of your home-coming."

"Dare you speak thus to *me*, knowing that this day the woman we both loved has died a horrible death at hangman's hands, and all for following the course *you* set and staked for her?"

"Nonsense, my friend. You have been deceived by a chance resemblance, if indeed any could exist between such wrinkles as were smoothed out today and a face that made the stars ashamed. I regret to say that I have lost sight of her for many a year—that maiden we both knew and loved; I would give all I have left to give to see her before me as she was. Her waist was slender as the waist of death—I cannot conceive her as blue flame and grey ash. Again, I say you have deceived yourself, my friend."

"Friend me no friends! What I feel for you is unscabbarded, naked hate."

"Death and the judgment! If you do not love me, you *fear* me, coward that you are!"

"Were I the crowning coward—the bye-word and mock of cowards— there would be one man beneath my fear."

"And do you mean that I am that man?" I challenge you then to accompany me to my castle. It is worth the seeing."

"You need not press me. I ask nothing better than your company. You shall tire of me ere I tire of you. Lead, and I will follow you to the fringes of the Pit."

"Well needs ride sabbatical post."

He plucked up two charred logs that lay near at hand. He thrust one between the knees of the galley-slave and the other between his own. He uttered a magic word, sharp, pungent, and obeyed. The logs became two stallions, black as grief and fleet as joy. Before Marquard had grasped the fact that he was mounted, they were out of the town,

The weather, as we have said, was of the clearest. A train of obscene hags, bound for some witches' frolic, was the only thing that rode the night. They passed it and left it easily in their rear. Their pace, in fact, was a pace to kill. They shook off a mile with every sweat drop. It took them a second to shoot through a forest. They cleared, not one river, but twos and threes at a time; the wind, striving to keep up with them, fell breathless. Huge mountains tossed their grandsire heads and deemed themselves impassable. These also the chargers crossed, and left them shrugging their fat shoulders far behind.

But now a peak of peaks appeared—a Babel that overlooked earth, and peered into heaven—would they double that? They reached its summit, but at the instant, with a word from the sorcerer, they were logs again.

Marquard reeled as his feet touched ground. He steadied himself with an effort, and took a step forward. The Hungarian seized him by the collar, just in time to save him from a fall. They were standing upon the edge of a precipice. The sailor looked down and saw no bottom—a gulf that staggered reason. He shuddered at his escape, and reeled again. When he had somewhat recovered, he rubbed his eyes, and took a careful survey of the position.

They had been deposited at the extreme altitude of the mountain. But it was not a single peak, it formed a ring like the crater of a volcano, but of a diameter so stupendous that its further side was barely visible to the naked eye. Of its depth we have already given some idea, but the most singular feature of the whole strange place—the feature which made it impossible to regard it as a mere giant volcano—was a slender spire of rock that shot up from its unknown floor to about the same height as the surrounding rim.

It might be compared to a Cleopatra's Needle set in a well, or else to the stamen of some egregious petrified flower. Or from the sailor's point of view (considering the spot where he stood as mainland) it was an islet left bare by a dried-up sea. Nor was it a desert island. It was inhabited, or at any rate it was built upon. There was a castle on it which it was just large enough to hold. The outer walls merged straight down as if one piece with the wall of rock upon which they were founded. From the front entrance, a bridge of marble, with rails of gold, spanned the abyss that separated the castle from the mountain.

While Marquard was making these observations, the Hungarian took stock of him with his single eye. When the sailor had apparently sucked in all his environment, Teremtette asked him, what seemed on the face of it, a needless question.

"What do you see?"

"I see a castle, whiter than a bride, uplift upon yon mast of stone."

"What else do you see?"

"I see a bridge across the airy moat that parts us from that fantastic crow's nest."

"That castle and that bridge are of my architecture. If you consider as child's play all that you *have* dared—if you are willing to *begin* to show high courage—you can follow me within its gates."

He walked towards the bridge, crossed it, and disappeared within the castle walls. The galley slave sat down, and gazed at the fairy fabric in something very much like indecision. He felt among his garments to see if he still possessed the talisman, the witch's parting gift. It was there. He drew it forth and looked at it. A little shrivelled pellet, of some unknown dried substance, it was as much of an enigma to him as ever. He laid it upon the rock on which he sat, and turned again towards the castle. To his horror and astonishment, it was losing its clearness of outline. It became—along with the bridge—semi-transparent. He could see through them both.

They grew thinner, and thinner. They faded into little more than mist. Ultimately nothing of either was any more visible. Only the bare pillar stood up in the midst of the chasm. But no—there was a figure upon the now tonsured rock—it was the figure of the Hungarian. A moment's thought explained this. The castle alone was unsubstantial. In disappearing it left revealed the man that had been within it. He was too far off for the sailor to be sure of what he was engaged on. There ran through all Marquard's veins a current of fear. He felt helpless in the presence of all this glamour that he did not understand. He looked round for his only friend—the amulet—thank God! it was still there. He snatched it up, resolved never more to let it away from him.

And then another wonderful thing occurred. The castle and its bridge again gradually appeared in sight. The sailor began to suspect the rules of the game. He could not forbear to put the talisman down again for a moment. The outlines of the magical buildings grew immediately dim. He took up the ball. Their solidity was immediately restored. He now knew his bearings. There could be no longer any doubt. Apart from their creator—the Hungarian—the castle and bridge were only visible to the holder of that wizened trifle. Marquard packed it away, with heightened respect, and deliberately walked up to, and across, the bridge. It rang substantial enough under his feet, for him to almost doubt the truth of what he had just seen. He was too near his enemy to hazard any more experiments.

He found him in a goodly, square, and most singularly wall-papered room, inasmuch as each of its walls—where not pierced for a door—was one vast mirror. In the centre stood a table loaded with every delicacy in and out of season. At each side of the table was placed a luxurious chair. The Hungarian pointed to one of these and spoke.

"I bid you to this last supper, in the name of those that hold this house, if you dare sit down and feast."

"I dare do anything in *your* company."

"Then eat, drink, and be merry, for tomorrow one of us two dies. That, I believe, was the intention, with which you accompanied me hither?"

"You are right therein, as always."

"Then for an hour we will proclaim a truce to all our differences. We will pledge the survivor in flowing bowls from vintages of a thousand years. Wine you shall have creating thirst and woman creating desire. That is if you can call *her* woman that tempted Adam out of Paradise."

"To whom do you refer?"

"To Lilith, Eve's rival, queen of all damnations!"

"Was it for her, then, that you sold your soul and swopped an eye with Satan?"

"Ha-ha, you have heard that story. It is true that I left my eye in pawn, but it is false that I received one in exchange. This is not an eye at all—this Evil Eye as they call it—whose beam is supposed to blight wherever it falls. In your own person you have tested its perfect harmlessness."

He paused, as if to see whether the sailor had swallowed this more than doubtful statement. The latter made no sign. The wizard then proceeded to lift his sinister eyelid, until the fiery stab of the Evil Eye was a second time unveiled. As before it had no effect whatever on Marquard. The magician then lifted his finger to it, and with a twist turned the apparent eye-ball out of its socket. It slipped over the finger that had released it, and in so doing shewed what it really was. It was a *ring* set with an enormous blazing stone!

Yes, this was the fabled Evil Eye, this innocent circlet of gold with its flashing stone. The magician obligingly extended the hand that now wore it, to the end that Marquard might examine it more minutely. As he got accustomed to its baleful glare, he perceived that this was not generated by the gem itself. The gem was hollow, and served merely as a receptacle for something alive that crouched within. From the eyes of this living weevil—or devil—or whatever it was—streamed the poison of ill-effect which the public had thought to proceed from an Evil Eye. Nor were they wrong after all, only that there were two evil eyes, and their owner to boot—instead of one.

But even this was only the beginning of the Hungarian's surprises. Having allowed the sailor to gaze long enough upon the ring, he rested the hand that wore it upon a chair. Then with the other hand he just touched the gem at his side. It flew open and the creature that lived in it came forth. She increased in size—the sailor saw that it was a woman—a woman, whose beauty would have blinded the severest eye. She would have seduced an anchorite to dimpled sin.

"You see," laughed the Hungarian, "that, if I got no eye from the devil, he gave me a rib out of his side."

When she had reached the height of her companion Lilith stopped growing, and sat down upon her chair. The magician seated himself at one hand of her, the sailor at the other, and looked inquiringly towards the vacant place that fronted her.

The Hungarian intercepted his glance, and grinned.

"Look at the mirror, man," he cried, "there are more guests here—and more august—than you imagine."

The galley-slave looked at the mirror behind the vacant side of the table, and started from his seat in sudden terror. The mirror reflected the back of someone as if occupying that chair, which nevertheless still stood in front of it, empty. The sailor looked from chair to mirror—from mirror to chair again—but there was no mistaking that weird fact. His hair stood up. He sank into his seat. He snatched to his white lips the first goblet that came to hand. The magician at once took up his own glass and cried out, mockingly,

"I second your toast! To the health of our guest—the Orb and Sceptre of all the hells!"

From that the orgie waxed fast and furious. They swam in music. The room was grey with incense. Their lights were balls of coloured fire that flashed in the air, and ever and *anon* dropping into their cups hissed like snapdragons. Songs were sung that fallen angels had brought from paradise. Tales were told of doings done before the world was planned. But who sung, and *who* narrated was beyond the sailor's ken, a-swim as he was with wine and witchery.

He grew more and more bemused. The table whirled round and round. The viands slipped away from his hands, when he turned to look at his fair neighbour, he could only find the one eye of the Hungarian. The mirrors gave back distortions. All was confusion and delusion, and mocking laughter in his ears. After a brave attempt to keep his head, he rolled upon the floor. The vintages of a thousand years had done their work.

When he awoke, with a splitting headache, the room was clear. The Hungarian paced up and down at one end. A glance at him sufficed to show that the matchless ring had been restored to its socket.

"Ha-ha," laughed the sorcerer, "are you looking for the girl you were so sweet on last night? Behold her!" He lifted his eyelid, and there flashed forth *coquettish* lights from the prisoner of the gem.

The sailor sprang to his feet.

"Arch and unheard-of juggler," he cried, "your play is played, and your curtain is nigh to ringing down. You have done the devil's work—beshrew the like!—and you shall get the devil's wages. You shall rue the day you brought me here."

"The nightmare be your bride! Were you not girt with an adverse fate you had dawned in a fiercer place than this! And now, if you are bent upon a duel—and the laws of hospitality do not protect me—I will even let you take the lead."

"Then look to yourself, witch-master!" cried the sailor, drawing a rusty pistol from his long sea-boot. He took aim, and fired; the bullet struck the Hungarian, and *rebounded*. A peal of laughter shook the hall.

"The devil kiss your lips!" cried the sorcerer; "you have no reach for me! But try again if you like before I set my foot on the neck of your revenge."

The sailor considered. It was no use wasting another leaden bullet on a man who was evidently impregnable to such. He remembered that a silver button cut from one's coat was considered sovereign against a wizard when all else failed. But, unfortunately, Marquard wore no silver buttons, and very few buttons of any kind. An idea struck him, there was the magic ball that the witch had given him. It was true that, if it flew wide of its mark, he would have staked, and lost, his all; since he would no longer boast any influence to protect him.

On the other hand, he felt a presentiment that it would not fail him. In any case the sorcerer, who was aware by this time of his possession of the talisman, seemed, from his good humour, to have forged some device by which he could counteract it. Marquard threw his scruples to the wind, and rammed the amulet into the pistol.

"I will bring your royal insolence a-dust," he cried "in hackneyed, unoriginal death for all that you are the devil's fetch and carry!"

He fired. Thunder shook the furthest stars. The room was full of foetid smoke. As it partially cleared away, the galley-slave saw his enemy lying supine upon the ground. He crept up to him, still misdoubting, and touched him gingerly. He was dead. But when Marquard came to look upon his face, he started back surprised, all trace of the ring had entirely disappeared. Both the sorcerer's eyes were open, and both were now a match. But whence had come back this long-lost eye? It was the ball Which the witch had handed over to Marquard—the ball which Marquard had loaded into his pistol—the ball which had steered unerring to its ancient seat, and ousted the usurper which it found there.

Marquard reverently lifted the fallen pride of Wizardry and carried him gently to the outer gate. This man upon whom he had served the warrant of that bowelless catch-poll—Death, this clay, after all was said and done, had once been boyhood like himself. Lovers of one girl the tunes of their two lives were built upon the same bottom note. It was with tenderness that Marquard tossed the body into the abyss. He did not know how soon he was to follow it. It had scarcely disappeared when he became aware from the thinning of the castle that he had unwittingly got rid of the power which enabled him to cross the bridge. The golden railing had already vanished. He started to run, but the marble under his feet was softening, and he sank in it to the ankles at every step.

A little further and his legs went through to the knee. With incredible exertions he reached the centre, but could go no further. He floundered in the fast ebbing material, hopelessly, to the waist. Then he sank to his armpits—spread out his arms so as to hold yet a second to life— but finally the last remnants of the bridge evaporated, and he fell plumb into the gulf, turning over and over in his fall.

The Witches' Sabbath

Our scene is one of those terrific peaks set apart by tradition as the trysting place of wizards and witches, and of every kind of folk that prefers dark to day.

It might have been Mount Elias, or the Brocken, associated with Doctor Faustus. It might have been the Horsel or Venusberg of Tannhaeuser, or the Black Forest. Enough that it was one of these.

Not a star wrinkled the brow of night. Only in the distance the twinkling lights of some town could be seen. Low down in the skirts of the mountain rode a knight, followed closely by his page. We say a knight, because he had once owned that distinction. But a wild and bloody youth had tarnished his ancient shield, the while it kept bright and busy his ancestral sword. Behold him now, little better than a highwayman. Latterly he had wandered from border to border, without finding where to rest his faithful steed. All authority was in arms against him; Hageck, the wild knight, was posted throughout Germany.

More money was set upon his head than had ever been put into his pocket. Pikemen and pistoliers had dispersed his following. None remained to him whom he could call his own, save this stripling who still rode sturdily at the tail of his horse. Him also, the outlaw had besought, even with tears, to abandon one so ostensibly cursed by stars and men. But in vain. The boy protested that he would have no home, save in his master's shadow.

They were an ill-assorted pair. The leader was all war-worn and weather-worn. Sin had marked him for its own and for the wages of sin. The page was young and slight, and marble pale. He would have looked more at home at the silken train of some great lady, than following at these heels from which the gilded spurs had long been hacked. Nevertheless, the music of the spheres themselves sings not more sweetly in accord than did these two hearts.

The wild knight, Hageck, had ascended the mountain as far as was possible to four-legged roadsters. Therefore, he reined in his horse and dismounted, and addressed his companion. His voice was now quite gentle, which on occasion could quench mutiny, and in due season dry up the taste of blood in the mouths of desperate men.

"Time is that we must part, Enno."

"Master, you told me we need never part."

"Let be, child, do you not understand me? I hope with your own heart's hope that we shall meet again tomorrow in this same tarrying place. But I have not brought you to so cursed a place without some object. When I say that we must part, I mean that you must take charge of our horses while I go further up the mountain upon business, which for your own sake you must never share."

"And is this your reading of the oath of our brotherhood which we swore together?"

"The oath of our brotherhood, I fear, was writ in water. You are, in fact, the only one of all my company that has kept faith with me. For that very reason I would not spare your neck from the halter, nor your limbs from the wheel. But also, for that very reason I will not set your immortal soul in jeopardy."

"My immortal soul! Is this business then unhallowed that you go upon? Now I remember me that this mountain at certain seasons is said to be haunted by evil spirits. Master, you also are bound by our oath to tell me all."

"You shall know all, Enno, were oaths even cheaper than they are. You have deserved by your devotion to be the confessor of your friend."

"Friend is no name for companionship such as ours. I am sure you would die for me. I believe I could die for you, Hageck."

"Enough, you have been more than brother to me. I had a brother once, after the fashion of this world, and it is his envious hand which has placed me where I stand. That was before I knew you, Enno, and it is some sweets in my cup at any rate, that had he not betrayed me I should never have known you. Nevertheless, you will admit that since he robbed me of the girl I loved, even your loyal heart is a poor set off for what fate and fraternity took from me. In fine, we both loved the same girl, but she loved me, and would have none of my brother. She was beautiful, Enno—how beautiful you can never guess that have not yet loved."

"I have never conceived any other love than that I bear you."

"Tush, boy, you know not what you say. But to return to my story. One day that I was walking with her my brother would have stabbed me. She threw herself between and was killed upon my breast."

He tore open his clothes at the throat and showed a great faded stain upon his skin.

"The hangman's brand shall fade," he cried, "ere that wash out. Accursed be the mother that bore me seeing that she also first bore him! The devil squat down with him in his resting, lie with him in his sleeping, as the devil has sat and slept with me every noon and night since that deed was done. Never give way to love of woman, Enno, lest you lose the one you love, and with her lose the balance of your life."

"Alas! Hageck, I fear I never shall."

"Since that miscalled day, blacker than any night, you know as well as any one the sort of death in life I led. I had the good or evil luck to fall in with some broken men like myself, fortune's foes and foes of all whom fortune cherishes, you among them. Red blood, red gold for a while ran through our fingers. Then a turn of the wheel, and, presto, my men are squandered to every wind that blows—I am a fugitive with a price upon my head!"

"And with one comrade whom, believe me, wealth is too poor to buy."

"A heart above rubies. Even so. To such alone would I confide my present purpose. You must know that my brother was a student of magic of no mean repute, and before we quarrelled had given me some insight into its mysteries. Now that I near the end of my tether I have summed up all the little I knew, and am resolved to make a desperate cast in this mountain of despair. In a word, I intend to hold converse with my dead sweetheart before I die. The devil shall help me to it for the love he bears me."

"You would invoke the enemy of all mankind?"

"Him and none other. Aye, shudder not, nor seek to turn me from it. I have gone over it again and again. The gates of Hell are set no firmer than this resolve."

"God keep Hell far from you when you call it!"

"I had feared my science was of too elementary an order to conduct an exorcism under any but the most favourable cir-cumstances. Hence our journey hither. This place is one of those where parliaments of evil are held, where dead and living meet on equal ground. Tonight, is the appointed night of one of these great Sabbaths. I propose to leave you here with the horses. I shall climb to the topmost peak, draw a circle that I may stand in for my defence, and with all the vehemence of love deferred, pray for my desire."

"May all good angels speed you!"

"Nay, I have broken with such. Your good wish, Enno, is enough."

"But did we not hear talk in the town about a hermit that spent his life upon the mountain top, atoning for some sin in day-long prayer and mortification? Can this evil fellowship of which you speak still hold its meetings upon a spot which has been attached in the name of Heaven by one good man?"

"Of this hermit I knew nothing until we reached the town. It was then too late to seek another workshop. Should what you say be correct, and this holy man have purged this plague spot, I can do no worse than pass the night with him, and return to you. But should the practices of witch and wizard continue as of yore, then the powers of evil shall draw my love to me, be she where she may. Aye, be it in that most secret nook of heaven where God retires when He would weep, and where even archangels are never suffered to tread."

"O all good go with you!"

"Farewell, Enno, and if I never return count my soul not so lost but what you may say a prayer for it now and again, when you have leisure."

"I will not outlive you!"

The passionate words were lost on Hageck, who had already climbed so far as to be out of hearing. He only knew vaguely that something was shouted to him, and waved his hand above his head for a reply. On and on he climbed. Time passed. The way grew harder. At last exhausted, but fed with inward exaltation, he reached the summit. It was of considerable extent and extremely uneven. The first thing our hero noticed was the cave of the hermit. It could be nothing else, although it was closed with an iron door. A new departure, thought Hageck to himself, as he hammered upon it with the pommel of his sword, for a hermit's cell to be locked in like a fortress.

"Open, friend," he cried, "in heaven's name, or in that of the other place if you like it better."

The noise came from within of a bar being removed. The door opened. It revealed a mere hole in the rock, though large enough, it is true, to hold a considerable number of persons. Furniture was conspicuous by its absence. There was no sign even of a bed, unless a coffin that grinned in one corner served the occupant's needs. A skull, a scourge, a crucifix, a knife for his food, what more does such a hermit want? His feet were bare, his head was tonsured, but his eyebrows were long and matted, and fell like a screen over burning maniacal eyes. A fanatic, every inch of him. He scrutinised the invader from top to toe. Apparently, the result was unsatisfactory. He frowned.

"A traveller," said he, "and at this unholy hour. Back, back, do you not know the sinister reputation of this time and place?"

"I know your reputation to be of the highest, reverend father; I could not credit what rumour circulates about this mountain top when I understood that one of such sanctity had taken up a perpetual abode here."

"My abode is fixed here for the very reason that it is a realm of untold horror. My task is to win back, if I can, to the dominion of the church this corner, which has been so long unloved that it cries aloud to God and man. This position of my own choice is no sinecure. Hither at stated times the full brunt of the Sabbath sweeps to its rendezvous. Here I defy the Sabbath. You see that mighty door?"

"I had wondered, but feared to ask, what purpose such a barrier could serve in such a miserable place."

"You may be glad to crouch behind it if you stay here much longer. At midnight, Legion, with all the swirl of all the hells at his back, will sweep this summit like a tornado. Were you of the stuff that never trembles, yet you shall hear such sounds as shall melt your backbone. Avoid hence while there is yet time."

"But you, if you remain here, why not I?"

"I remain here as a penance for a crime I did, a crime which almost takes prisoner my reason, so different was it from the crime I set out to do, so deadly death to all my hopes. I am on my knees throughout the whole duration of this pandemonium that I tell you of, and count thick and fast my beads during the whole time. Did I cease for one second to pray, that second would be my last. The roof of my cavern would descend and efface body and soul. But you, what would you do here?"

"I seek my own ends, for which I am fully prepared. To confer with a shade from the other world I place my own soul in jeopardy. For the short time that must elapse, before the hour arrives when I can work, I ask but a trifle of your light and fire.

"The will-o'-the-wisp be your light, Saint Anthony's your fire! Do you not recognise me?"

The wild knight bent forward and gazed into the hermit's inmost eye, then started back, and would have fallen had his head not struck the iron door. This recalled him to his senses, and after a moment he stood firm again, and murmured between his teeth, "My brother!"

"Your brother," repeated the holy man, "your brother, whose sweetheart you stole and drove me to madness and crime."

"I drove you to no madness, I drove you to no crime. The madness, the crime you expiate here, were all of your own making. She loved me, and me alone—you shed her blood, by accident I confess, yet you shed it, and not all the prayers of your lifetime can gather up one drop of it. What soaked into my own brain remains there for ever, though I have sought to wash it out with an ocean of other men's blood."

"And I," replied the hermit, and he tore his coarse frock off his shoulders, "I have sought to drown it with an ocean of my own."

He spoke truth. Blood still oozed from his naked flesh, ploughed into furrows by the scourge.

"You, that have committed so many murders," he continued, "and who have reproached me so bitterly for one, all the curses of your dying victims, all the curses I showered upon you before I became reformed have not availed to send you yet to the gibbet or to the wheel. You are one that, like the basil plant, grows ever the rifer for cursing. I remember I tried to lame you, after you left home, by driving a rusty nail into one of your footsteps, but the charm refused to work. You were never the worse for it that I could hear. They say the devil's children have the devil's luck. Yet some day shall death trip up your heels."

"Peace, peace," cried the wild horseman, "let ill-will be dead between us, and the bitterness of death be passed, as befits your sacred calling. Even if I see her for one moment tonight, by the aid of the science you once taught me, will you not see her for eternity in heaven some near day?"

"In heaven," cried the hermit, "do I want to see her in heaven? On earth would I gladly see her again and account that moment cheap if weighed against my newly discovered soul! But that can never be. Not the art you speak of, not all the dark powers which move men to sin, can restore her to either of us as she was that day. And she loved you. She died to save you. You have nothing to complain of. But to me she was like some chaste impossible star."

"I loved her most," muttered the outlaw.

"You loved her most," screamed the hermit. "Hell sit upon your eyes! Put it to the test. Look around. Do you see anything of her here?"

115

The other Hageck gazed eagerly round the cave, but without fixing upon anything.

"I see nothing," he was forced to confess.

The hermit seized the skull and held it in front of his eyes.

"This is her dear head," he cried, "fairer far than living red and white to me!"

The wild knight recoiled with a gasp of horror, snatched the ghastly relic from the hand of his brother, and hurled it over the precipice. He put his fingers over his eyes and fell to shaking like an aspen. For a moment the hermit scarcely seemed to grasp his loss. Then with a howl of rage he seized his brother by the throat.

"You have murdered her," he shrieked in tones scarcely recognisable, "she will be dashed to a hundred pieces by such a fall!"

He threw the outlaw to the ground and, retreating to his cave, slammed the door behind him, but his heartbroken sobs could still be heard distinctly. It was very evident that he was no longer in his right mind. The wild knight rose somewhat painfully and limped to a little distance where he perceived a favourable spot for erecting his circle. The sobbing of the crazed hermit presently ceased. He was aware that his rival had entered upon his operations. The hermit re-opened his door that he might more clearly catch the sound of what his foe was engaged upon. Every step was of an absorbing interest to the solitary as to the man who made it.

Anon the hermit started to his feet. He fancied he heard another voice replying to his brother. Yes, it was a voice he seemed to know. He rushed out of the cave. A girlish figure clad in a stained dress was clasped in his brother's arms. Kiss after kiss the wild knight was showering upon brow, and eye, and cheek, and lip. The girl responded as the hermit had surely seen her do once before. He flew to his cave. He grasped the knife he used for his food. He darted like an arrow upon the startled pair. The woman tried to throw herself in front of her lover, but the hermit with a coarse laugh, "Not twice the dagger seeks the same breast," plunged it into the heart of her companion. The wild knight threw up his arms and without a cry fell to the ground. The girl uttered a shriek that seemed to rive the skies and flung herself across her dead. The hermit gazed at it stupidly and rubbed his eyes. He seemed like one dazed, but slowly recovering his senses. Suddenly he started, came as it were to himself, and pulled the girl by the shoulder.

"We have not a minute to lose," he cried, "the great Sabbath is all but due. If his body remains out here one second after the stroke of twelve, his soul will be lost to all eternity. It will be snatched by the fiends who even now are bound to it. Do you not see yon shadowy hosts—but I forget, you are not a witch."

"I see nothing," she replied, sullenly, rising up and peering round. The night was clear, but starless.

"I have been a wizard," he answered, "and once a wizard always a wizard, though I now fight upon the other side. Take my hand and you will see."

She took his hand, and screamed as she did so. For at the instant there became visible to her these clouds of loathsome beings that were speeding thither from every point of the compass. Warlock, and witch, and wizard rode post on every conceivable graceless mount. Their motion was like the lightning of heaven, and their varied cries—owlet hoot, caterwaul, dragon-shout—the horn of the Wild Hunter, and the hurly of risen dead—vied with the bay of Cerberus to the seldseen moon. A forest of whips was flourished aloft. The whirr of wings raised dozing echoes. The accustomed mountain shook and shivered like a jelly, with the fear of their onset.

The girl dropped his hand and immediately lost the power of seeing them. She had learned at any rate that what he said was true.

"Help me to carry the body to the cave," cried he, and in a moment, it was done. The corpse was placed in the coffin of his murderer. Then the hermit crashed his door to its place. Up went bolts and bars. Some loose rocks that were probably the hermit's chairs and tables were rolled up to afford additional security.

"And now," demanded the man, "now that we have a moment of breathing space, tell me what woman-kind are you

117

whom I find here with my brother? That you are not her I
know (woe is me that I have good reason to know) yet you are
as like her as any flower that blows. I loved her, and I murdered
her, and I have the right to ask, who and what are you that come
to disturb my peace?"

"I am her sister."

"Her sister! Yes, I remember you. You were a child in those
days. Neither I nor my brother (God rest his soul!), neither of
us noticed you."

"No, he never took much notice of me. Yet I loved him as
well as she did."

"You, too, loved him," whispered the hermit, as if to himself;
"what did he do to be loved by two such women?"

"Yes, I loved him, though he never knew it, but I may confess
it now, for you are a priest of a sort, are you not, you that shrive
with steel?"

"You are bitter, like your sister. She was always so with me."

"I owe you my story," she replied more gently; "when she
died and he fell into evil courses and went adrift with bad companions, I found I could not live without him, nor with anyone
else, and I determined to become one of them. I dressed in boy's
clothes and sought enlistment into his company of free lances.
He would have driven me from him, saying it was no work for
such as I, yet at last I wheedled it from him. I think there was
something in my face (all undeveloped as it was and stained with
walnut juice) that reminded him of her he had lost. I followed
him faithfully through good and evil, cringing for a look or
word from him. We were at last broken up (as you know) and I
alone of all his sworn riders remained to staunch his wounds. He
brought me hither that he might wager all the soul that was left
to him on the chance of evoking her spirit.

"I had with me the dress my sister died in, that I had cherished through all my wanderings, as my sole reminder of her life
and death. I put it on after he had left me, and followed him as
fast as my strength would allow me. My object was to beguile
him with what sorry pleasure I could, while at the same time
saving him from committing the sin of disturbing the dead. God

forgive me if there was mixed with it the wholly selfish yearning to be kissed by him once, only once, in my true character as loving woman, rid of my hated disguise! I have had my desire, and it has turned to apples of Sodom on my lips. You are right. All we can do now is to preserve his soul alive."

She fell on her knees beside the coffin. The hermit pressed his crucifix into her hands.

"Pray!" he cried, and at the same moment the distant clock struck twelve. There came a rush of feet, a thunder at the iron door, the cave rocked like a ship's cabin abruptly launched into the trough of a storm. An infernal whooping and hallooing filled the air outside, mixed with it imprecations that made the strong man blanch. The banner of Destruction was unfurled. All the horned heads were upon them. Thrones and Dominions, Virtues, Princes, Powers. All hell was loose that night, and the outskirts of Hell.

The siege had begun. The hermit told his beads with feverish rapidity. One Latin prayer after another rolled off his tongue in drops of sweat. The girl, to whom these were unintelligible, tried in vain to think of prayers. All she could say, as she pressed the Christ to her lips, was "Lord of my life! My Love." She scarcely heard the hurly-burly that raged outside. Crash after crash resounded against the door, but good steel tempered with holy water is bad to beat. Showers of small pieces of rock fell from the ceiling and the cave was soon filled with dust. Peals of hellish cachinnation resounded after each unsuccessful attempt to break down that defence. Living battering rams pressed it hard, dragon's spur, serpent's coil, cloven hoof, foot of clay. Tall Iniquities set their backs to it, names of terror, girt with earthquake.

All the swart crew dashed their huge bulk against it, rakehelly riders, humans and superhumans, sin and its paymasters. The winds well-nigh split their sides with hounding of them on. Evil stars in their courses fought against it. The seas threw up their dead. Haunted houses were no more haunted that night. Graveyards steamed. Gibbets were empty. The ghoul left, his half-gnawn corpse, the vampire his victim's throat. Buried treasures rose to earth's surface that their ghostly guardians might swell the fray. Yet the hermit prayed on, and the woman wept, and the door kept its face to the foe. Will the hour of release never strike? Crested Satans now lead the van. Even steel cannot hold out for ever against those in whose veins instead of blood, runs fire. At last it bends ever so little, and the devilish hubbub is increased tenfold.

"Should they break open the door—" yelled the hermit, making a trumpet of his hands, yet she could not hear what he shouted above the abominable din, nor had he time to complete his instructions. For the door did give, and that suddenly, with a clang that was heard from far off in the town, and made many a *burgher* think the last trump had come. The rocks that had been rolled against the door flew off in every direction, and a surging host—and the horror of it was that they were invisible to the girl—swept in.

The hermit tore his rosary asunder, and scattered the loose beads in the faces of the fiends.

"Hold fast the corpse!" he yelled, as he was trampled underfoot, and this time he made himself heard. The girl seized the long hair of her lover pressed it convulsively, and swooned.

Years afterwards (as it seemed to her) she awakened and found the chamber still as death, and—yes—this was the hair of death which she still clutched in her dead hand. She kissed it a hundred times before it brought back to her where she was and what had passed. She looked round then for the hermit. He, poor man, was lying as if also dead. But when she could bring herself to release her hoarded treasure, she speedily brought him to some sort of consciousness. He sat up, not without difficulty, and looked around. But his mind, already halfway to madness, had been totally overturned by what had occurred that woeful night.

"We have saved his soul between us," she cried. "What do I not owe you for standing by me in that fell hour?"

He regarded her in evident perplexity. "I cannot think how you come to be wearing that bloodstained dress of hers," was all he replied.

"I have told you," she said, gently, "but you have forgotten that I cherished it through all my wanderings as my sole memento of her glorious death. She laid down the last drop of her blood for him. She chose the better part. But I! my God! what in the world is to become of me?"

"I had a memento of her once," he muttered. "I had her beautiful head, but I have lost it."

"That settles it," she said, "you shall cut off mine."

The Devil's Debt

Somewhere about the Middle Ages—somewhere in a medi-aeval town—there lived a man who walked always on the shady side of the way. None of his neighbours could have assigned a reason why he should only tread where the lapse of time leaves no trace on the dial, yet so it was. None had ever seen him in sunshine.

This man was known by the name of Porphyro, though we may reasonably doubt if it was given to him in baptism. For he belonged to a class that baptised toads by night at their Sabbaths in mockery of the baptism of babes by day. In a word, Porphyro was a wizard, and for one circumstance (which will presently be mentioned) was perhaps better known among his like than any practiser of the Black Art before or since.

There was, and likely enough still is, in Europe a University of the occult sciences, buried underground, carved out of the roots of mountains, far from the hum of men. Here taught weird professors—eerie, eldritch, elflocked. Here came weird students to tread the intoxicating wine-press of magical study. Your true wizard is set apart from birth by some particularity which be-speaks his vocation. To the University came representatives of every class which felt this call. Here was the demoniac and the stigmatic, the abortion and the albino, the hermaphrodite and the changeling, the hag-ridden and the pixy-led, sleep-walker, Cesarean, Sunday-child, seventh son, and he that is born with the caul. This motley crew was of as many hues as there are ends of the earth. Many tongued as Mithridates, all wrote their notes by common consent in the *lingua angelorum*.

The university boasted a laboratory of at least a hundred paces in length and proportionately broad and high. A mock sun gave it cold light by day, and a mock moon by night. Here experiments in exorcism were conducted, of course under the strictest supervision of the principals. Here the students learned that the ghosts of dead men (having, always some of the old Adam that was unpurged from them), are easier to call back to us than elemental spirits can be wrenched from their eternal spheres. The most trivial task (and therefore that of the junior classes), was to re-incarnate some suicide, set in four cross roads, whose soul still hovered like a noxious gas about the only body where it could hope to find toleration. The pupils were very properly forbidden to incur the danger of repeating these experiments in private.

Nevertheless, something of the kind went on under the rose. As a rule, the novices (and these were after all the lucky ones), ignominiously failed in their attempts to storm the outworks of hell. They knew how to call, spirits from the vasty deep, but the spirits refused to come when they did call them. One youth, however, boasted that he had raised the devil, or at any rate, a devil. He described him to his bosom friends nearly as follows:—

"A great and full stature, soft and phlegmatic, of colour like a black obscure cloud, having a swollen countenance, with eyes red and full of water, a bald head, and teeth like a wild boar."

One of the listeners, doubtless jealous, attempted to cheapen this success of his companion, by remarking that an exorcist, if worth his salt, should be able to make the spirit appear in what guise he chose.

"Then, by the belt of Venus," swore a third, " I would command it to appear as a lovely girl, with longer hair and smaller feet than any on this top, which the Almighty set spinning and dubbed earths. Another poor fellow appears to have been so inflamed with the suggestion of this rustler, that he tried to bring it into the sphere of practical politics. He was never seen alive again. Not answering to his name at the roll-call next morning, his bedroom was visited, and a thin trickle of blood found oozing under the door. One of the search party put a pistol to the lock and fired. The door flew open.

A cry burst from all present, and some of the youngest, covering their faces with their hands, fled. The body of the devoted wretch who had played with unholy fire, was scattered parcel meal about the room. The lopped limbs were twisted round into spirals as if boneless. One of stronger stomach than the rest of the onlookers, and who examined them more closely, declared that the bone had melted and run out under some incredible heat. One of the teachers opined that if the demon had only breathed upon the bone, it would have been enough to fuse it. There were no more experiments in students' rooms.

Apart from such accidental deaths, the Academy paid a regular yearly rent of one living soul to hell, and woe unto teachers and taught had they lapsed into arrear one day. The victim who was to suffer, that the rest might live and learn, was selected in the following traditional manner. The whole of the pupils toed a line at one extreme end of the hall, and, at a given signal, raced to the opposite door. There was, as may be imagined, a terrible struggle to pass through the hangings. The last to cross the threshold was hugged to hell by the awaiting fiend.

It was on such an occasion that Porphyro earned the unique distinction, alluded to above, of having successfully cozened the Prince of Darkness himself. Strain as he might, he was the last to touch the winning post. His competitors, who now breathed themselves in safety in the lobby, had given him up for lost. But no piercing shriek of dissolution stabbed the air, no fiendish laughter made horrible the echoes. Instead, voices were heard, until presently their comrade rejoined those who had already mourned him. Amid a scene of the wildest excitement, he was dragged into the light. Something unprecedented must obviously have occurred. His hair had turned snowy white. Those fell back who looked first into his eyes, for they saw in them reflected the face of Hell himself.

The tale which Porphyro told them was in substance this, that when he arrived last at the curtains, and; already felt the breath of punishment upon his cheek, there occurred to him one loophole of escape. He turned desperately at bay, like hunted quarry, and roundly told the scrutineer that all he could claim by the letter of his bond was Porphyro's shadow. That was the last living thing which passed out of the lists; and not Porphyro, who preceded it. Strange as it may seem, after a few heated words, the justice of this quibble was acknowledged by the father of all such juggleries. He bore off the shadow with a sort of smile, that was more terrible than men's frown, and lo and behold! when the schoolfellows, with one accord, looked down at the feet of him who had so miraculously escaped the infernal maw, they saw that Porphyro was, as he ever afterwards remained, shadowless. And now our readers can guess why our hero walked always on the shady side of the way.

Nothing had ever been known (even in circles like this) so successfully daring as this piece of evasion. Round and round the whole round globe, by means only known to wizards, the news sped fast to all the wizard world. It was proclaimed at every Sabbath, from Blockula to the Brocken. The Lapland witch whispered it to the Finland witch, as they sat tying up wind after wind in knots for their seafaring, customers.

The Druids of Carnac knew it, and the Persian devil worshippers. The Shamans of Siberia made a song of it and beat their magic drums thereto. The magicians of Egypt pictured it in their mirrors of ink. The African Obi men washed their great fetish in the blood of a thousand virgins, and sent it as a present, over the desert sands, to Porphyro. Even the medicine men heard of it in the heart of an undiscovered continent, and emblazoned it upon the walls of their medicine lodge.

Everyone foresaw a brilliant career for Porphyro. They fully expected him to disembowel Hell. The reverse was what really happened; Instead of swinging himself at once to the top round of the ladder, he showed no disposition to trouble himself at all. He opened a private office in the town referred to at the beginning of our story, and carried on a private business in magic of the whitest kind. For him no monster evocations, with a million demons at his beck and call, like the Sicilian whom Benvenuto Cellini employed to conjure for him in the Coliseum.

Porphyro refused in the most stiff-necked manner to exorcise on any terms for anyone. He confined himself solely to petty-fogging business, such as writing talismans, and reckoning magic squares, drawing horoscopes, and casting schemes of geomancy, poisoning rivals for lovers, or closefisted relatives for spendthrift heirs. Need we state in black and white the reason (concealed from everyone else), why he held his hand from higher things? Oh! the humiliation of it! He was afraid! Yes, Porphyro was afraid, even he, who had plucked a hair from the devil's beard, for that very reason he was afraid. He had saved his soul alive, losing only a shadow of little moment to him, but in return, he had incurred the eternal enmity of one whose grudge had once shaken the high heavens.

The general adversary of all mankind was first and beyond all things most ferociously Porphyro's adversary. Unhappy Porphyro, who had already given seisin to hell, Porphyro with one half of him already in the living devil's clutch, who never slept but he dreamed of the tortures his poor shadow suffered at the hands of those that lovingly work evil! Tortures, which were but foreshadowings of his own! No wonder Porphyro dared not invoke even the least of spirits. He knew too well that the mightiest of them would appear with no greater calling than a word.

But there was one antidote which wrestled with the night-shade in his cup, one star of the right colour appeared above his horizon. There was a woman in his town (one only for him) a princess and the ward of a king, an exquisite beauty. From the first time he saw her, he loved her with a passion which reproached his meaner self. She fed upon his sighs, without knowing that the air she breathed was full of them. In any case, he would never have dared to speak to her. It was sufficient daily bread to him to see her move. He hung upon her footsteps. He, kept pace with her in her rides, running ever in the shadow because he himself had no shadow to call his own.

Yet he forgot while looking at her this one great fact, of his life. Even in his dreams she presently held his hand while he suffered. And he dreamed of her thus till he set his teeth in his pillow. Gradually her little mouth sucked up all the breath of his body. He wrote poems about his princess and swallowed them. Often, he took no other food for days. He made philtres which would infallibly have caused her to love him, had he not ruthlessly thrown them all away as soon as made. He constructed an image, of her in wax, and worshipped it five times daily. It was this which wrought his downfall. Certain of his clients (they had not paid him) denounced him as a sorcerer. Without notice he received a domiciliary visit from the authorities.

Apart from other evidence which the house contained, the wax image of the princess was discovered, and he was at once charged with intending to make away with her life. Oh, the irony, of fate, he who would have cheerfully laid down his own for her! Being forcibly removed from his house, the secret he had so long kept was discovered, and this shadowlessness, though accounted for in a hundred ways, all wide of the truth, was added at once to the long list of crimes in his indictment. At the preliminary examination, he would confess nothing. He was accordingly imprisoned pending the preparation of tortures to shake his resolution. With the aid of these refinements, he might be made to confess anything, even that he had attempted the life of his best beloved. The scaffold loomed before him. And oh, that her name should be bandied about in such context.

Meanwhile Porphyro sat, body and soul in darkness. He saw none but the jailer, who brought him food once daily, with a finger ever on his lips. Rats there were, and such small deer, but with these he could hold no converse, although in his youth he had met with men who professed to teach their languages, Porphyro was fain to chatter constantly to himself that he might have no time to think. He played his school games over again, rehearsed his school tasks to imaginary masters, held imaginary conversations with clients and with his parents long dead, and with his princess who was more than parent, and more than dead to him.

He wooed her in a thousand ways, now as an emperor, raising her to his level, now as the meanest of her grooms, to whom she sweetly condescended, now he was a soldier, better vised to red lips of wounds than red lips which wound, now he was a scholar, who forgot all wisdom save hers, now he was a miser, who came like Jupiter, in a shower of gold. Thus, riotous reigned carnival before his coming Lent.

And now comes the strangest part of all this strange eventful history. He fancied once or twice that he was replied to as he spoke. Again, and again he groped all over the blind prison, and felt no one Yet there was of a surety a tongue which answered him. And the weirdness of it was that, turn though he might, it always spoke from behind him. Again, he searched the litter of the dungeon, and again without result. The voice was at first unintelligible, like the murmur of the sea, yet with a cadence which soon struck his ear as strangely familiar. He had heard it only once before, but it had been in that cock-pit underground where he had fought a main which had coloured his whole life. He was bound up with the memory of it like a poor prisoner whom men fetter to a corpse. It was the still small voice which dominates the brawl of Hell.

His hair could grow no whiter, else it had done so. He listened with all his ears and began to catch syllables and afterwards words, till at last he made out that the Tempter was proposing terms of peace with him.

Right well knew Porphyro (none better), the price that must be paid for such a truce. His soul must feed the quick of Hell. It seemed hard to yield up at last that immortal henchman which he had once so gloriously saved from these same talons.; Yet what chance had he? On the one hand, if he maintained his feud with the Evil One, the halter was weaving which must strangle love and life. On the other part, if he surrendered his soul to the Exile, he could at any rate make what terms he pleased. And there were terms he pictured himself exacting which made ultimate payment of the highest price seem easy to the blood which had once stood face, to face with Satan, and given him better than he gave. Porphyro still continued to argue *pro* and *con*, though his decision was a foregone conclusion. At last he formulated his demands to the spirit. He must marry the princess. He must be her husband, were it but for a single night.

The walls of the dungeon suddenly became bright with a

kind of phosphorescent glow. Porphyro (still alone, or, at any rate, he seemed so) saw a table standing in front of him, bearing a bond already drawn and the materials for signing it. The terms set forth were those he had himself proposed. He signed, sealed, and delivered it, and was plunged into darkness again as his finger left the parchment. A sense of infernal laughter pervaded the air, though nothing was to be heard. Porphyro fell full length to the ground in a fainting fit. When he recovered his jailer was standing over him, come (as he thought) to bring him food, but he was soon disabused of any such notion by the man himself. He, who had refused on all prior occasions to hold converse with his prisoner, now spoke voluntarily to tell him the sands of his captivity had run out.

At first the dazed cage bird (who had forgotten for the moment his compact) believed that he was on the point of expiating his crimes, real and imaginary, upon the scaffold. But the jailer, not without difficulty, made it clear to him that all captives received pardon on the joyous occasion of the marriage of their princess, which was fixed for that day. Then Porphyro remembered all, and swooned again.

When he revived, our hero was sitting in the open air upon the steps which led from the jail. He caught the smell of oxen roasting whole in the market-place. The sky was red with the fires. The streets as far as he could see them, were paved with flowers and, decorated with triumphal arches. The citizens were bustling about in holiday attire. Music seemed to be playing everywhere. Occasionally some exuberant person fired off a gun. Porphyro rubbed his eyes and wondered whether this could really be his wedding day. He had faith in the boundless powers of the banner under which he had enrolled himself. And yet was it possible? But his faith was amply justified.

An equerry suddenly rode up, parting the spectators to right and left, leading a spare horse magnificently caparisoned, and followed in the distance by a brilliant retinue. He doffed his cap to Porphyro and sprang to the ground, and with a profound obeisance, said in tones of deep respect:—

"I trust Your Highness has recovered from your indisposition.

I have brought the horse as Your Highness commanded."

Porphyro dimly understood that some potent influence was at work on his behalf. With the assistance of his squire he took to the saddle. The latter then, with another bow, remounted his own horse, scattered a handful of gold to each side to break up the crowd, and with the rest of the train (which had caught up with them) they galloped to the cathedral. Porphyro noted with stupid surprise that all the fountains spouted wine, whereto certain of the citizens, judging by the hiccups which mingled with their cheers, had already applied themselves, not wisely but too well. But our hero was in a state of so great fog himself as to feel his heart warm more towards these than to the soberer ones, whose salutations he clumsily returned.

By the time the cathedral was reached, he was rolling in his saddle. He could not have dismounted without help. The incense made him dizzy. He could not get the ringing of the bells out of his ears. The candles danced before his eyes. Of all the service he heard one word, and that was uttered by one who stood beside him, and whom alone he saw (and that through a mist) of all that gay assembly. It was the princess. He pressed her hand as if he would never part with it.

The service over, he had no idea how, or in what order they reached the castle, and the banquet which followed was more or less of a blank to him. The wines of which he partook liberally, could make him no more drunk, nor all the compliments of all the fulsome speeches (had he heard them) raise by one degree his pride. He soared empyrean high in the thought that he had won the right to crush into one cup, one moment, all the eternal delirium of all the heavens.

That moment of fruition had come at last. Porphyro stood in that holy of holies, his princess's chamber. A guard of soldiers was ranged along the four walls of this dainty nest. Each leaned with one arm upon a pike, while with the other hand he held aloft a blazing torch. Great personages were also present, both courtiers and noble dames, and at last the bride herself was brought in by her women. While complimentary discourse passed from mouth to mouth, Porphyro longed with his whole bartered soul to be alone with her. He was burning with internal fire which he could hold in little longer. At last he approached one that appeared to act as master of the ceremonies.

"When is this rigmarole going to end?" he muttered between his teeth.

"Whenever Your Highness pleases to draw your sword and lay it in the middle of the bed, the princess will take up her place upon one side of it, while you occupy the other," was the reply.

Porphyro started. He surely recognised that voice. The official kept his face averted, but it was undoubtedly the demon.

"What mean you by this gabble of naked swords between me and her?" thundered Porphyro, unheeding who might hear. "Damned posture master, is she not my wife?"

"Your wife, yes, but only by letters of procuration," and there was a note of triumph in that voice.

"God of the Judgment! What is that you say?"

"I say you must be dreaming not to remember that you are only temporarily united to the princess in your character of proxy for His Imperial Majesty, the Holy Roman Emperor"

"Alas the while! Then I am dreaming, indeed!"

"These soldiers," continued the demon, "will remain here all night. These ladies and gentlemen will also attend here till morning, to entertain you and your bride of an hour through your somewhat tedious spell of lying fully dressed together."

"Death and the Pit! Is this true?"

"True as death, assured as the pit. Tomorrow you will sheathe your sword, and depart from her for ever."

Porphyro pressed his hands to his temples. He thought his brain would burst. He saw it all now. He was the dupe of the fiend who had once been his dupe. His place in this pageant had been contrived with infernal subtlety, only to wring the uttermost pang from his heart strings. He who sups with the devil (they say) must needs have a very long spoon. No help was possible. The Evil One was reaping his revenge. And now he was assured his victim had at last grasped the situation, he threw off the mask, and showed himself in his true colours. He raised his eyes for the first time from the ground, those brimming lakes, of bottomless hate which Porphyro had fronted once before in the underground hall. It was his turn now to quail.

"Ha! ha!" laughed the fallen angel. "By mine ancient seat in heaven (and that is an oath I never lightly take as you may guess), confess, have, I not rested you, friend Porphyro? He laughs best who laughs the last; is it not so?"

"But what about that bond registered between us in Hell's chancery?" cried Porphyro, in a voice which would have melted triple brass.

"Your bond," shrieked Beelzebub. "Do you remind me of your bond; you who once outfaced me that a bond should be read by the letter, and not by the spirit? I have come round to your views, and I now fling that word back in your teeth. You have had your bond to the letter, and now go and kill yourself, for there is nothing more for you to do."

Porphyro bent like a broken reed. He had found his over-mastering fate. His hopes were ash. He breathed in gasps. He staggered to the window, and threw open the casement. A great pitiful star looked in, but to his eyes it appeared red and blood-shot. He turned round again to the room. He wished to see once more before he died that mistress of his soul for whose sake, he had flung it away. But the figure of his master had swelled, and was swelling so rapidly in size that it seemed to fill every available corner of the room.

Porphyro raised his hands to heaven, and called upon his lady's name. Three times he called it, and then sprang out of the window. The princess, who had grasped nothing of what had passed, ran to the shutter, and looked out just in time to hear the splash of his body as it fell into the moat. It was the first sign of interest in him which she had shown.

LEONAUR

ALSO FROM LEONAUR
AVAILABLE IN SOFTCOVER OR HARDCOVER WITH DUST JACKET

MR MUKERJI'S GHOSTS *by S. Mukerji*—Supernatural tales from the British Raj period by India's Ghost story collector.

KIPLINGS GHOSTS *by Rudyard Kipling*—Twelve stories of Ghosts, Hauntings, Curses, Werewolves & Magic.

THE COLLECTED SUPERNATURAL AND WEIRD FICTION OF WASHINGTON IRVING: VOLUME 1 *by Washington Irving*—Including one novel 'A History of New York', and nine short stories of the Strange and Unusual.

THE COLLECTED SUPERNATURAL AND WEIRD FICTION OF WASHINGTON IRVING: VOLUME 2 *by Washington Irving*—Including three novelettes 'The Legend of the Sleepy Hollow', 'Dolph Heyliger', 'The Adventure of the Black Fisherman' and thirty-two short stories of the Strange and Unusual.

THE COLLECTED SUPERNATURAL AND WEIRD FICTION OF JOHN KENDRICK BANGS: VOLUME 1 *by John Kendrick Bangs*—Including one novel 'Toppleton's Client or A Spirit in Exile', and ten short stories of the Strange and Unusual.

THE COLLECTED SUPERNATURAL AND WEIRD FICTION OF JOHN KENDRICK BANGS: VOLUME 2 *by John Kendrick Bangs*—Including four novellas 'A House-Boat on the Styx', 'The Pursuit of the House-Boat', 'The Enchanted Typewriter' and 'Mr. Munchausen' of the Strange and Unusual.

THE COLLECTED SUPERNATURAL AND WEIRD FICTION OF JOHN KENDRICK BANGS: VOLUME 3 *by John Kendrick Bangs*—Including twor novellas 'Olympian Nights', 'Roger Camerden: A Strange Story', and ten short stories of the Strange and Unusual.

THE COLLECTED SUPERNATURAL AND WEIRD FICTION OF MARY SHELLEY: VOLUME 1 *by Mary Shelley*—Including one novel 'Frankenstein or the Modern Prometheus', and fourteen short stories of the Strange and Unusual.

THE COLLECTED SUPERNATURAL AND WEIRD FICTION OF MARY SHELLEY: VOLUME 2 *by Mary Shelley*—Including one novel 'The Last Man', and three short stories of the Strange and Unusual.

THE COLLECTED SUPERNATURAL AND WEIRD FICTION OF AMELIA B. EDWARDS *by Amelia B. Edwards*—Contains two novelettes 'Monsieur Maurice', and 'The Discovery of the Treasure Isles', one ballad 'A Legend of Boisguilbert' and seventeen short stories to cill the blood.